# THE GIRL
# THAT GLOWS

## by ONYX

To
My Daddy!
I Love You
with all of my heart!
You are my favorite
person in the world!
Onyx

The Girl That Glows ©2016
by Onyx

ISBN 13:  978-1-365-13846-1

First Printing May 2016
Printed in the United States of America

Fiction:Urban:Contemporary:Memoir
10 9 8 7 6 5 4 3 2 1

To Sandra Stanley

and the women who come through
Opening Doors For Women In Need

## Prelude

The puke green walls are the first thing I see when I open my eyes. My head hurts. My face is lying on the cold concrete floor. Where am I? My hands are handcuffed behind my back. I feel like my shoulder is about to pop out of socket. I wish somebody would come take these handcuffs off.

"Hey. Can anybody hear me? Hey." I hear a loud voice from the next cell all of a sudden yell out,

"Girl you might as well be quiet. We can all hear you, but nobody gives a damn what you got to say."

"Who said that?" I try to sit up, but the room starts spinning so I lay back down. I close my eyes and try to get myself together before I speak.

" Do you think somebody will come take these cuffs off? They're too tight, and my arm hurts really bad."

"Look girl we all got problems, and right now my biggest one is a headache that ain't getting no better with you screaming your head off. They will come take off the cuffs when they feel like it.

You in jail, so all you got is time. Just chill out." Jail?JAIL??

How did I get here? Oh I remember....

I guess I should go back to the beginning. I mean wayyyy back to where it all started...... I have been somewhere like this before. Not jail, but worse. A long time ago. The memories crawl up my spine, across my chest and grab my throat......

Chapter 1

"Connie. Connie. I know you hear me. Get cho skinny, little, black, nappy- headed self back here."

"Please Ma don't make me do nothing. It hurts so bad. I'll be good. I promise."

"Shut up. It ain't that bad. You know I need my medicine."

Mama snatches me to her and pushes me in the room. The man sitting on the bed has on a blue suit, and he even smells good. Maybe he has a little girl like me and won't hurt me.

"Come ere baby. You sho is a pretty lil' thang. Come sit on my lap. My name is Mr. Johnson."

I slowly walk over to the bed so that I can see his eyes. Their eyes always tell me if they going to hurt me. Yep. His eyes are squinted, and his mouth is hanging open just a little bit. My palms start to sweat, and I start to fart real loud. He frowns up his nose I know that it must have smelled pretty bad, but right then I couldn't help it. I'm in trouble.

Then he says, "That's right come 'ere. I just want to hug you for a little while."

When I get close to him he reaches out and grabs me. Puts me right on his lap. He starts rubbing my arms, and squeezing me real, real tight.

"Oh yeah. It's alright I got something real nice fo' you." Then he pulls down my shorts and rubs his thing all over my booty. I don't cry because that only makes it worse. I think they like it when I cry. After it's all over I lie down on the bed and wait fo my mama to come get me.

"See that wasn't so bad huh? Look what he gave me to give you."

I raise my head and open my eyes. A brand new shiny quarter. Maybe it wasn't so bad after all.

"Come on gal and get back in yo room. I got a date." "Okay ma, but please don't make me get in the box. It's scary in the box."I don't like the box. I even hate to talk about the box. It is made for dogs, and they don't even like it.

"Come on ugly ass girl. I ain't got all night to be playing with you." Sometimes going in the box was harder than others. It has metal bars so I can see out. Dogs don't even like being in these things, and momma say they're made for them. As soon as I'm about to fall off to sleep I hear mama calling my name.

"Connie. Wake up girl, somebody here to see you." I look at the window in my room and see that it's still dark outside, so I know it's somebody bad."

"Now Connie don't make no fuss and it be ova quick."

I open my eyes and see that it's the tall white man with the red hat. I really start crying now 'cause I know this is gonna be real bad. He looks at me with this big ole smile. "Hey Connie. It's been a while huh?"

I'm really crying hard now, cause I know he is gonna stick his thing in my pee-pee hole until he pee white stuff all over me.

Crying don't matter, or don't cry don't matter. He still gonna hurt me real bad. As he picks me up I try to go someplace else in my mind. I know that he can do anything he wants to my body, but nobody lives in my mind but me. In my mind I can go anyplace I want and nobody can hurt me. I go to my favorite place. My big momma's kitchen. There is always a lot of food to eat, and the only other person there is my big momma. She really loves me. It don't matter that I'm black, or that my hair is nappy. Big mama...

"Connie get up and go wash that blood off of you. Then get back to your room to yo' box."

I was only 6 years old. Why is all this stuff happening to me? I have a little brother and nothing happens to him. He has a real bed in his room with toys, and everything. I guess mama is right. I'm a bad person because I'm so black. Maybe I can wash this black off. I know we have some bleach here. Maybe the stuff mama uses to wash the dishes with will wash this black off of me.

"Connie. Why do I smell all that bleach? What are you doing? I thought I told you to get back in yo' box."

Please mama. Ima get this black off. Just wait a minute it's coming off.

"Girl what chu doing? Why are you wasting my stuff? Ain't nothing gon' get that black off. You gon always be black, and you gon always be ugly."

She leans down, squints her eyes and points her finger in my face.

"Now get to yo room, and get yo butt in that box."(Slap.)

"Okay ma. I'm sorry. I'm going. Don't hit me."

She pushes me  to the ground, and begins to kick me. The more I scream the more she kicks. The bleach has spilled on the floor and she holds my face down in it.

"You little black girl. Do you think the black is coming off now?"

I just scream, and try to keep my mouth closed. I know she will get tired soon. She always hits and kicks me until she runs out of breath.

I wonder why God  made me this way? He must hate me too.

I can feel my li'l brother Michaels' warm body pressed up against my box. He's holding on to my fingers. It must be morning. He always wakes up laying right here. He should be in his warm soft bed instead of laying here next to me. In his own way I think he loves me. He always stares at me and holds my fingers every morning. He has beautiful light brown skin and I wish I looked just like him. I guess I'm just glad that he doesn't have to live like me.

"Connie I'm hungry."

"Go tell momma. She will give you something to eat." "Why are you in there? Were you bad?"

"Michael I guess I was just born bad. Just be glad that you weren't."

"What's all that noise in there? Michael what are you doing in there? You better stay out of there. I don't know how many times I'm going to have to tell you that. Stay away from that thang."

I just start to cry, because my little brother is the only good thing in my life. Now she is taking that away too.

I just lay down and wish I lived far away with a mommy and daddy who loved me even though I'm so black. I would have my own toys to play with and my own bed. I would also have lots of brothers and sisters. They would all love me so much. My big mama would always come for a visit, and the kitchen would smell so good.....

I wonder how long I was asleep? It's still light outside. I can even hear kids playing. Mama never lets me go outside anymore. Maybe when we have school again. I will get to go. Even though the kids make fun of me I still like to watch them play too....

"Now get up and get ready for school. I don't want them people coming to my house."

I get to go to school today. Yeah!..... I only have one other dress to wear and it's dirty too, but cleaner than this one. As I get ready to walk out the door.....

"You know what goes on in this house stays in this house, 'cause I will find you and I will kill you."

"I know mama I ain't gonna tell."

As I'm walking down the street to the school a group of girls walk past me I hear one of them say,

"You so black, you blacker than the bottom of my shoe." All the other girls laugh.

Then I hear,"You so black, you block out the sun."I look at the little girl, and she has the meanest look on her face.

I just put my head down, and keep walking. This boy comes up behind, and pushes me to the ground. My dress flies up. A little boy runs up behind me.

"Ugh. You nasty. You ain't got no panties on." All the kids surround me and laugh and call me names. I just lay there curled up in a ball hoping they will go away.

"What are you guys doing over there? Who is that on the ground?"

I look up, and see the most beautiful woman in the world. She has the lightest skin I've ever seen besides white people. Her hair is real black, but very straight and very long. Her eyes are green and look like cats eyes. She squats and softly says

"Hello. What's your name? Please get up off the ground, and come inside with me. My name is Mrs. Sneed. I'm a teacher here."

She has on a real pretty green dress, and she has a nice smile. I get up off the ground.

"Hi my name Connie." She must be new here 'cause I've never seen anybody that looks like her at this school.

"Well Connie it's nice to meet you. Who is your teacher?" I didn't know what to say. I didn't really know her name. All I can remember is that she was very mean to me. "I 'ont know" I begin to shift from one foot to the other. I am so nervous.

"Do you know what grade you are in?"

"Yeah, 1$^{st}$ grade." All of a sudden her face lit up like a Christmas tree.

"I'm your teacher then."

I am so excited. I have a teacher, and she is light and beautiful. I just know things are going to get better for me. That day school time fflies by. Soon it is time for me to go home.

"Mrs. Sneed? do you want me to wipe off the blackboard for you?"

"Sure Connie, and would you mind picking up those toys in the corner for me?"

"No ma'am. I'll do it." I took my time 'cause I really didn't want to go home.

"Uh Connie? Would you please come here after you're finished? I want to talk to you about something."

Just hearing those words make me so nervous that I almost drop all the toys that I had picked up all over the floor. My palms and armpits get all sweaty. My stomach just starts turning over and over. Oh man. What did I do wrong today? I'll bet she wants some light skinned kid to help her after school. Anybody, but my black ugly self.

"Yes Mrs.Sneed what did I do? I can do better just give me a chance."

"You didn't do anything wrong Connie. I want to talk to you about your dress. Does your mother know what you wore to school today?"She sits down in one of the chairs at the childrens' table. Her voice drops to almost a whisper. "Do you have better clothes at home to wear?"

"No. My mama don't have no money for clothes. She has to buy her medicine."

Mrs.Sneed gently grabs my hand.

"Well do you think your mama would mind if I bought you some clothes to wear to school?"If my face could have gotten red. It would have then. I am so embarrassed. Yet, happy all the same.

"I don't know. I don't think so."

"I'm going to bring you some tomorrow okay?"

"Okay Mrs.Sneed. I better go home now. I'll see you tomorrow." All I could think about is what Mrs.Sneed is going to bring me to wear tomorrow. I am so excited that I forget to knock on our door. I just walk right on in. Mama is sitting on the couch with her head down, and a needle stuck in her arm. I know she has just had her medicine, and might be kind of nice for a while. "Mama. Mama. I'm home. I got a new teacher, and she says that she is gonna bring me some clothes to school tomorrow. Mama is that okay?"Mama slowly opens her eyes,and glares at me. Then she sneers,

"Don't you ever bother me when I'm sleep off my medicine. I don't care about no new teacher. If you bring any clothes in my house that I ain't bought , I will set yo' lil black behind on fire."

She picks me up, and throws me back down to the ground. I get up and run to my room. I curl up into a ball, and try to go to my special place in my mind. My big mommas' kitchen. That's the only way to make myself feel better when it hurts so bad.

* * *

The next morning I am so sad. How am I going to tell Mrs.Sneed that my mama wouldn't let me take the clothes? I am dragging my feet the whole 2 blocks there. Once I get on the school grounds this boy named Paul yells out,

"Hey blackie. What are you doing coming to school 2 days in a row?" Other kids began to surround us. "Like my momma say I know it's gonna rain now. You better stay away from me, 'cause you gon' turn into a big puddle of mud. Ha-Ha."

"Paul. That is not very nice. I want you to apologize right now."

"I ain't not. She is black. And she is ugly. My momma  say she ain't nothing but throwed away garbage."He takes off running across the school yard.

"Oh Connie I'm so sorry. I can go get him and make him apologize."

"No. That's okay. I'm used to it any ole ways. It don't even bother me no more." My hands starts shaking. I am so nervous. "Mrs.Sneed my mama say I can't get no clothes from you. Please don't be mad at me." I take in a big breath, and wait for her to yell at me.

"But Connie why? I don't want anything for them."

"My mama said no."I turn away. I don't even want to look down to avoid her sad face.

"What if you just kept them here at school? She wouldn't even have to know." I had never thought about that. That is a great idea.

\* \* \*

That night as I am going off to sleep I keep thinking about all the pretty clothes I am going to have at school. I couldn't wait til tomorrow. Maybe I'll get a red dress....

\* \* \*

"Dog. Wake up. We gotta go."

I crawl out the box and stand up. I am afraid, because she has never taken me anywhere before.

"Come on girl I ain't got all day."

Maybe she is taking me to big mommas' house. Oh goody. I'm hungry too. I climb into the back seat, and we take off. I am so excited to be driving in a car I can hardly keep my face off the side window. When we turn on to the highway I really get confused, but I am not saying nothing. This ride is fun. After riding for about an hour Mama turns into this drive way.

What is this place I just see a lot of doors. "Wait right here."

I'm standing outside beside one of the doors. I don't know what's going on,or even why I'm here. Uh-oh the door is opening.

"Git on in here girl. Now you be nice to Mr. Charlie. You better do whatever you're told to do. I'll be right outside in the car."

Laying on the bed is this real black man. Shoot he blacker than me, so I know that he is real bad.

"Look girl, I'm telling you this now. I ain't wit all that cryin' and stuff. Just come 'ere, and do what I say."

The things that happened to me in that place I will never forget. I try to go away in my mind, but I couldn't. He just keeps dragging my mind, and body all over that room. I think that day I finally realize that the devil isn't in some far away place for people who did bad things, but he was right here and his face was blacker than mine.

When my mama finally came back I was laying in the corner wishing I was dead. Whatever that was.

"Baby go stand outside the door and wait for mama. I'll be out there in a minute."

I walked outside and noticed that it was raining. I wondered why I couldn't even cry anymore. Even the sky could cry. I watched the sky cry for me all night. My mama didn't come out until the morning.

My li'l brother Michael, and I love to play in mamas' room inside her closest. She has so many shoes. We make shoe forts, shoe people, shoe cars, shoe everything. One day my lil brother and I are in the closet playing, and somebody shut the door and turned off the light. I try to open the door, but I can't so I sit down on the floor. Michael gets scared and starts to cry, but not me. I am use to the dark. I pull him onto my lap and hug him real tight. We stay in that closet for a long time. We go to sleep and woke up so many times I lose count. All I remember is after a long while my big momma opens the door.

## Chapter 2

Living at my big mommas' house was crazy. Every day, all day my mama comes and bangs on the doors. Telling my big momma she wants her baby back. I don't get it. Michael isn't here. He went to live with his daddy, and I know she doesn't want me. She hates me. Told me that all the time. She once told me she don't know why they want me instead of her. I wasn't nothing and never would be nothing. I always wonder what she meant. I wish somebody would tell her Michael isn't here, so she will go away.

\* \* \*

One morning, big mama says,"Baby you know I love you with all my heart, but I can't keep dealing with your mama."

"Just tell her Michael ain't here, and she will go away."

"Child she knows Michael ain't here. It's not Michael she wants. It's you."

"No. Please big mama  don't make me go with her. I don't want to. "

"But why? That's yo' mama. She say them drugs made her lock you, and Michael in that closet. She says she ain't takin them drugs no more. She wants me to tell them white people that she should have her kids back."

"I don't want to go back. Please big mama. Don't make me.

I can't bring myself to tell my big mama about all the things that my mama did to me, 'cause I am too scared. Also, I am ashamed. I feel  like if my big mama know about some of the things she would think I am bad too.

My big mama didn't make me go back, but she couldn't deal with my mama neither, so I had to leave. Michael's daddy wants me to come live with him like my little brother, but the judge says since he isn't my daddy I can't go. So since they can't find nobody to take me I end up going to the juvenile home.

It isn't a bad place. They feed you, and you have your own room. Plus, nobody cares if you are light or dark. They hate all of us. All except this one staff name Mrs. Knight. She has dark skin like me, but she is really pretty, and she likes me because I know how to sing. Yes I may have been black as night, but I can sing like an angel. All the years I have been going through all that stuff when things got real bad I would open my mouth, and sing. Sometimes I would look up from my bed while I am singing, and see Mrs. Knight  standing there listening. "Please don't stop singing Connie. Your voice is so beautiful. Who taught you all those church songs?"

"My grand-daddy is a preacher, and I have been singing at church since I was a baby." I really wish she would get away from my door. I didn't do anything.

"You know they tell me that you haven't done anything wrong to be here. They just didn't have anywhere to put you. How long have you been here?" I roll my eyes,'cause I know she knows the answer to this  question

"Well I was 7 when I came, and now I'm 11. So I guess that means 4 years."I know that she can tell that I am irritated by her presense.

"You know I have an idea. You guys have so much talent here. I mean you can sing, Kiesha can dance, some of the boys can rap. We should have a talent show."

"Mrs.Knight that sounds like a good idea, but we are kids who nobody cares about. Nobody is gonna want to see a talent show put on by us. Believe me." I sit up on the side of my bed, and drop my head.

"Yes they will. As long as I can get the other kids to do it, and you guys keep up your school work and chores." I jump up, and my eyes buck wide open. "Wow. Mrs. Knight do you really think so?"

"Connie of course I do. You just do your part. Do you think you can help me get the other kids to do it?" I crack up then. I am laughing so hard I bend over holding my stomach. "Please, you're not going to be able to stop them from trying to be in it once they hear about it."

* * *

"Connie, is it true that Mrs. Knight is gonna have a talent show?"

"Yeah it's true, and I already know that you want to dance in it Kiesha."

"Shoot girl I'ma win with my moves. I know you think you are the new black Diana Ross.

Ha-Ha, and you are gonna win, but you're not."

"Girl you is so stupid. I don't think I'm gonna win, but I don't think you are either. You dance like a white girl." I roll my eyes, and shake my head. Soon we are surrounded by lots of kids. "Hey what chall arguing about?"

"Mrs. Knight is having a talent show, and she wants all of us to be in it. Of course dummy here thinks she gon' win."

"Staight up? It's about time we have some fun around here." Everybody starts to talk at once.

"So all y'all will be in it?" The kids start to jump up and down, and I can feel the excitement in the air.

"Yeah. Yeah."

\* \* \*

"Mrs. Knight. Mrs. Knight everybody says they will be in the show." I am out of breath. I had to run to catch up with her.

"That's great Connie. Tell everybody to pick out what they want to do, and on y'alls free time practice. Plus, I'll try to get y'all some more practice time too okay?" She stops walking, and turns around and looks down at me.

"Okay Ms. Knight. Can I be your assist?" I didn't want to ask for anything. I know she won't want anyone like me.

"Why of course Connie you're my assistant. I'll even get you a clipboard okay?" I can't believe it. She wants me to help. She wants me.

"Yes Mrs. Knight I won't let you down."

We have a whole show ready. We have singers, dances, skits, and mini fashion show. I mean we are really ready.

\* \* \*

Well one evening, Mr. Townsend comes up to me. He is the evening supervisor, and he is really mean.

"Connie I see that you are a regular organizer here. I wonder if you can organize something for me."

I have met quite a few men like him in my young life, so I know what he wants. I follow him in the office. As soon as the door closes I start to take down my pants. He starts laughing and stops me.

He said "Look I don't want you. You ain't got no shape. Plus you too black. What I want you to do is set up something for me with sweet Kiesha, and any other girls in here or that come in here set it up so that they know what's up. Alright? If you can do this for me I'll make sure you got a few dollars in your pocket, plus keep the radio on in your room how is that?"

I thought about it. Can I set other girls up to go through that? Shoot, half of them are doing it to the boys in the bathroom anyway. They probably won't mind. Will I get pizza, or McDonald's on the weekend? "Yeah, if you pay for it out your own money. Don't try to push it girl." I sit back on the chair inside Mr. Townsends' office.

"Okay, okay deal." As I walk out of the office everybody is watching me with pity in their eyes, 'cause everybody knows how mean Mr. Townsend is, and they're wondering what I did to get in trouble. I got straight to my room, and as luck would have it Kiesha follows me. "Hey blackie what chu do now? You always in trouble."

"I didn't do nothing just leave me alone." I flop down on my bed. See I know how nosy she is, and I know I can probably talk her into meeting Mr. Townsend if she thought she could get in all my business.

"Come on girl. You might as well tell me what chu did, 'cause everybody gon' know by tomorrow anyway." She props up against the door-frame.

"No they won't cause this really is a secret and I can't tell nobody. It didn't work anyway." Now she stands up straight. This is just like fishing. They swim around the bait then finally put it in their mouth, and I get them.

"Ooh girl tell me. What chu do? You know I ain't gon tell nobody." She is jumping up and down now. That is a shame that she is so nosey. I get up, and go pull her into my room.

"Kiesha you promise you won't tell nobody?" I push her until she is sitting on my bed.

"Well I tried to do it to Mr. Townsend." She starts laughing so hard that she falls back on my bed holding her sides. She sits back up. Then says,

"Ha-Ha. Girl. You black as dirt, and you know you ain't got no booty. Why would you think he would want to do it to somebody that look like you? .Ha-Ha" She falls back over.

"Well now you can stop laughing 'cause I know that now. I was just trying to get some extra stuff. Somebody told me that would work." I roll my eyes up into my head, and fold my arms across my chest.

"Ha-Ha. Not with you though. Now you know." She is actually rolling around my bed cracking up.

"Yeah keep laughing, and I won't tell you what else I know." That is all it took for me to say. She sits up.

"I'm sorry girl. Tell me. What chu know?"

"Well... there is somebody that Mr. Townsend want to do it to." She jumps up, and puts her hands on her hips.

"Who?Who?Girl  you know you better tell me who it is." I turn away like I'm not going to tell her then quickly turn back around "You promise not to say nothing?" She grabs both of my arms she wants to know so bad.

"Yes. I promise. Tell me." I pause for a minute.

"You"

"Me.?Girl that is nasty.A grown man.?" I step up to her, and stare right into her eyes.

"I don't know what's so nasty about it. You done did it to every boy here, and you ain't get nothing out of it. I don't know why you wouldn't do it to get something." I point my finger right in her face.

"Well what do you think he will give me? Plus, won't it hurt?"

"Girl naw. As much as you do it." I step back, cause I almost laugh in her face.

"Okay go tell him I'll do it" It is like watching a movie as a I watch her face go from undecided to acceptance.

"Okay, but girl you better not chicken out on me at the last minute." I get ready to walk out the door, and stop to say something to her. I think better of it after a minute.

"I ain't. Go do it right now." I just look at her. She has no idea what she is getting herself into.

"Okay go wait in the storage closet."

* * *

"Well you wanted Kiesha? You got her. She waiting in the storage closet." Mr. Townsend is so excited he knocks his chair over.

"What. Already? Are you playing?" Why would he think I would into his office, and tell him something like that if I was playing around?

"No now give me my money." He put a 10 dollar bill in my hand, and almost ran out of the office.

* * *

The next morning Kiesha comes to my room.

"Hey Connie thanks girl he gave me 5 dollars."

"You so stupid. He gave me...um nothing girl that's cool. So you gon do it again?" I am laying down, but I have to sit up to listen to this foolishness.

"Probably, that's easy money baby."

* * *

Later while we are   practicing for the show I noticed a lot of the men staff are watching. I didn't pay it any attention until Mr. Townsend calls me over to him.

,"Connie, check this out. I want you to set something up for me okay?" I smack my lips, and put my hands on my hips.

"What do you want ? Ain't Kiesha enough for you? I thought you wanted her so bad?" I couldn't even imagine what he wants.

"Shut up girl. I want to hook my boys up." Now,I know he is tripping. What in the world did he expect me to do?

"Now you know Kiesha ain't gon do it to all those grown men." All he can think about is himself. What does he want me to do.

"Naw, naw girl I ain't talking about that. Kiesha mine. She special."

"What you mean is she cheap. You know you wrong for only giving that girl 5 dollars." I shook my head at him.

"Look, I asked her what she wanted, and that's what she said,so how I'm wrong?" I really roll my eyes then.

"Whatever. What you want me to do now?"

"Well I was telling somebody about my sweet little hook up here, and they said I....I mean we can make a lot of money here." I can see in his eyes the greed in his heart.

"Un-huh how?" I am really nervous now.

"Well... we could hook up other guys here with somebody, and have them give me... I mean us the money." I hear how he is somehow trying to leave me out of the equation already.

" I don't know about that... the other girls might not go for it. Especially if they ain't getting nothing." Honestly I could care less about those other girls, but I want to get something out of it today.

"Well how about if we give them stuff like candy, gum, pizza, McDonalds, pop, cigarettes, and joints?" He is staying there, and I can just see the wheels turning in his mind.

Well that might work, but I don't think I want to do this. Plus, I'm getting really busy helping Mrs. Knight with the talent show." His eyes begin to squint a little as He was getting upset more and more.

"If you don't help me I'll make sure there won't be a talent show."

Man. What have I got myself into now? All the kids will be crushed if we don't have this talent show, plus I promised Mrs.Knight I wouldn't let her down. I guess I don't have no choice.

Chapter 3

"Mr. Townsend. Mr.Townsend. Come here for a minute." He is walking passed the rec yard, and I run up to the fence.

"If you don't want to talk about what I think you want to talk about you're going to the quiet room for 72 hours for all that yelling."

"Oh come on now Mr.Townsend I know how you do. I wouldn't step to you unless I coming correct. Now tell me what's the plan? What do you need me to do? And most of all how much do I get paid and when do I get paid?"

"Well we are gonna use the last room down the hall. When one of my boys pick out a girl that he wants then it's your job to make sure she gets to that room at the right time. Then after it's done you will get 10 dollars every 'time. Oh, if somebody wants a boy it's gonna be your job to get him down the girls hall."

"Wait a minute. A boy? I don't know about that. I don't think I can get one of the boys to do it." I couldn't believe he had the nerve to say that. I start blinking my eyes faster and faster.

"Yes you can. Get one of the little ones. Besides we haven't come to that bridge yet." Oh my goddness. He is serious.

"Alright. When do we start?" I may as well go with the flow.

"Well... I have somebody who is looking at that new high yella fat girl. She should do it for a couple slices of pizza. This will be your easiest 10 dollars yet. Ha-Ha. Have her in the room at 5:30 during dinner time. Tell her not to worry she'll get something to eat."

* * *

The kids in the dayroom were yelling. The tv is too loud as usual. I spot the new girl over in the corner.

"Hey new girl. Come here for a minute so I can talk to you."

"What do you want? I ain't got nothing, so ain't no need to beat me up."

"Oh girl don't nobody want to beat you up. I just need to tell you something."

"Okay. What do you want?" The girl is looking scared to death as I approach her.

"Look all us girls here have a secret club. Do you want to be in it? If you do you can never tell nobody. Plus, if you're in it I promise you that nobody will ever beat you up. We get all kinds of extra special stuff. We get to stay up late on the weekends and everything. "I try to make what is going on sound fun.

"Yes girl yes. What do I got to do to be in this club?" She looks so excited finally. She really wants to fit in. Now I actually feel bad.

"Well, have you ever did it before?" She has no idea what she is getting ready to get into.

"Did what?" She looks at me like she really is interested in what I am saying.

"You know let a boy get on top of you, and stick his thing in." She almost jumps back when I say that.

"Oh girl no I ain't ever did that. That's nasty."

"Shut up. You talking too loud. That's okay if you don't want to be in our club. We having pizza tonight, and I don't want to share mine anyway." I turn to walk away. She stops me before I actually take 5 steps

"Wait a minute... They gon' give y'all pizza tonight? In here?"

"Yeah girl it gon have pepperoni, sausage, bacon, extra cheese uum... I can't wait." I begin rubbing my hands across my belly in circles. The look on my face is one of complete expectation.

"Y'all gon get a whole one by yourself?" Slob is practically running down her chin.

"Yep. They getting ready to order them now. "Wait a minute tell them to order me one too. Now tell me what I gotta do?" The excitement that is on her face in the beginning is beginning to fade.

"First of all you can't be no scardey cat. All you got to do is go in that last room, and sit down on the bed and wait. Somebody will come in and tell you what to do." She really begins to look nervous now.

"Is it gon hurt?" With wringing hands and buck eyes she asks,

"Probably just a little that first time, but after that you get used to it."

Things are going good for a while. After our talent show I am really busy trying to keep that room down the hall occupied all the time. I have more money than any 11 year old probably should ever even know about. Then Amy comes. She is a real little 9 year old red head white girl. She has only been there two days before Mr.Townsend comes to see me.

"Get the white girl in the room by 6 tonight."

"Aw man Mr.Townsend she too little, plus she cries all the time anyway. What am I supposed to tell that little girl to get her to go in that room?" I'm almost pleading. I don't want anything to happen that little girl.

"I don't care what you tell her. All I know is that she better be in that room at 6 tonight, or your tail is hit."

I went to my room to sit down and think. Amy was just too little. She even acts like a baby. How am I going to explain doing it to her? The only thing that I know she wants is her mommy. They say a pimp killed her mama. I wonder what a pimp is? Dang. This is gonna mess that little girl up. No it ain't. It happened to me when I was littler than her, and I'm alright. I see her sitting in front of the TV with her thumb in her mouth.

"Hi Amy. How are you doing?" When she sees me standing over her she says,

"I want my mommy." After she says that she starts to cry.

"Stop crying okay? It's gonna be okay. Do you want some candy?" I hold out my arms so that I can pick her up. I can tell that she is used to being treated like a baby.

"No. I want my mommy." I squeeze her tight to my thin chest. She rests her head on my shoulder.

"Look, come on let's go to this room down here, and you sit on the bed and wait a minute. Somebody is going to take you to your mommy." As we are walking down the hall towards the back room I begin stroking her hair.

"Really? I feel so bad she really believes me.

"Yeah. Come on. Let's go." Now I feel bad about tricking this little girl, and I didn't even warn her about what was gonna happen to her. Too late now. It's only my job to get them to the room then they have to take care of the rest.

"Connie. Connie. Wake up girl. They found Amy in that end room with no clothes on and she dead girl."

"What? Angie what are you talking about? Move outta my way." I run to the hallway and see a lot of staff going in and out of that end room, and all the other girls are just standing in their doorways crying. I am in shock. I am trying to figure out if I saw who went into that room with Amy earlier. I don't know who it was, but I know that I am gonna be in a lot of trouble if one of these dumb girls tell that I am the one who took that girl to that room. Why is this happening? It's not supposed to be like this. Nobody was supposed to get hurt. I didn't mean for anybody to get hurt.

"Get up girl. You going with me."

"Mr.Townsend. What happened to Amy?"

"How in the hell I'm supposed to know? I don't know nothing about that dead little white girl you hear me?

Now come on." He is almost pulling along.

"Where am I going?" I'm not even dressed.

"I unlocked the doors going down to the basement. You go down there, and climb out that window in the rec. room."

"Where am I going? I'm only 11 years old. I don't know where to go." I pull back to try, and stop him from walking.

"Just wait for me to get off work, and I'll take you somewhere." The look that he has on his face is one that I will never forget.

"No. I'm scared. I don't know where to wait for you." I can tell that he finally notices that I am afraid, because he softens his tone. "Just wait for me by the garbage cans. Don't let nobody see you either."

I just run out to the hallway. Everybody is worried about the room at the end of the hallway, so nobody even pays me any attention as I run across the dayroom,  open the door and run down the stairs. Dang it. I forgot my money.

Well too late to go back now. I have to break the window in the rec. room to get out it. It's so dark out here. How am I going to find the garbage cans? I think they are in the back somewhere. Here they are. I'm scared I hope he hurries up.

* * *

"Alright, this is the police. Come out with your hands where we can see them."

"Wait. Please. I'm only a kid I didn't do nothing. Please. I promise I didn't do nothing. I came out the juvenile home. I'm scared. Please." The policeman shines his light directly in my face.

"What are you doing out here by yourself?" Once he notices that I actually am a kid he softens his voice a little.

"Mr. Townsend told me to wait for him out here by the garbage cans. I didn't know where to go by myself. I'm just a kid." They put me in the back of the police car, and I am so scared. There are police cars everywhere. I just wish I could go back to my big mommas' kitchen. A policeman got in the car and we take off." Where am I going? Are you gonna take me too my big mommas house?" I am talking a mile a minute I'm so nervous.

"No. I'm not little girl. I don't know where your big momma lives. I'm taking you somewhere safe. Somewhere where people will take care of you."

We drove for a long time, and stop at this big house. We go up to the door, and knock. The door opens, and this little old white lady is standing there.

"Hello officer. Is this little Connie here?" She looks down at me, and I almost fall for her act. Something about her eyes tells me to wait.

"Yes ma'am. She's pretty scared, and very tired I'm sure." The officer almost pushes me into her arms. I can tell that he just wants to be rid of me himself.

"I'm sure she is. We'll take it from here officer. I'll take good care of her."

The policeman just walked away. He didn't say good-bye or nothing. The little old lady grabs me, and pulls me into the house. At first the smell takes my breath away. Then there are kids everywhere.

"Look gal, my name is Grandma Mabel. This here is my house, and what I say goes. Don't go in my kitchen unless you cleaning it, and never go in my front room. Tina here will show you where you sleep."

I couldn't believe it. Every time somebody took me somewhere it is worse than the last place. "What's your name nigger? You must be real bad 'cause they brought you here at night. They didn't have nowhere else to take you. Well let me tell you right now that I run this place, not grandma Mabel. You better do everything I say, or you will be sleeping outside in the garage with the dogs understand?"

First of all my name is Connie. I ain't no nigger, and Ima do whatever I want to do." I had been in the juvenile home a long time, and know that bigger kids will try to boss you around if you let them. Plus, I know that I can fight, so I am not worried about her one bit.

"Well Ms. I'll do whatever I want. You sleep down there by the wall. Maybe you'll learn your place after a while." I look at the bottom bunk and see the puddle of pee in the middle of the bed that is leaking down from the top bunk. I crawl right into the middle of it, and close my eyes.

## Chapter 4

In the morning the room I am in didn't look any better. If anything it looks worse. There are 4 bunkbeds filled with kids. The whole room smells like pee and something much worse.

"Alright brats. It's time to get up."

I look at the doorway, and the big white girl Tina is standing in the doorway yelling. Some of the little kids wake up crying, but everybody else just gets up and files out of the room. I just follow everybody down the stairs. There is a big room with lots of tables pushed together. I notice all the black kids sit at the tables in the back corner, so I go there too." We don't have much milk, so some of yall gon' have to put water in your cereal."

I know that meant us. I ain't hungry anyway, so I get up and begin to walk out of the room.

"Hey. Black girl. Since you're not going to eat breakfast you might as well start on your chores."

"Alright. What I got to do?"

"Wellll... since I'm sure this is gonna be your new room. Why don't you sweep up all that dog poop, and garbage in the garage. After you do those things then just hose it all down real good. The water hose right out back, but oh be careful. The dogs love little smart mouth black girls like you." She has both of her hands on her hips, and stares me up and down.

"Girl you must be crazy. I ain't going out there messing with them dogs."

"Ha-Ha. I was just playing. ... It's either that, or scrub every one of those pissy mattresses upstairs."

"Fine. Just give me a bucket and something to clean them with."

"Ain't no buckets in this house. You better use the bathtub, and one of them towels out the bathroom."

As I am walking out the of the room I bump right into grandma Mabel. Behind her is this really tall lady. "Chile watch where you are going. This here is detective Greer, and she wants to talk to you." I look up at the smiling tall black lady looking down at me.

"Hello Connie it looks like you guys are having breakfast. Are you still hungry? How about let's go grab some pancakes?"

"Can I have syrup on them too?"

"Why sure. As much as you like." I am so happy that I am jumping up and down.

"Okay. Let's go. We ran out of milk anyway." Grandma Mabels  face turns beet red, but we walk right out the door.

I kind of feel bad, 'cause I know that I smell like pee, and I want this lady to know right away that it isn't my fault.

"Look Ms. Greer I know I smell like pee, but I don't pee the bed. The bed they gave me to sleep in already had pee in it."

"That's okay Connie let's just go eat. I'm starving."

I am starting to like this lady already. When we get to the restaurant Ms.Greer tells me that I can have anything that I want.

"I just want some pancakes with lots of syrup. Oh. Can I have some milk too?"

She just smiles. Goes to order our food, then we go to our table. Ms. Greer looks at me for a minute then she says,"Tell me about Mr. Townsend at the juvenile home." I put my head down, and say,

"do we have to talk about him? Is he coming here to see me?"

Suddenly I am afraid. I didn't want to be like little Amy. "No Connie. Mr.Townsend is not coming here. He is in jail. He can't hurt you."

I just sit there, and look at her for a while. Then I start to cry. It has been so long since I could cry I didn't think I would be able to stop, but finally I did.

"He didn't want me. He said I was too black. He wanted me to get other girls to go in the room." My head is hung low, and I am speaking really softly.

"Was he the only grown up to go in the room?"

"I don't know. I would make sure the girl he picked out was in there, then I would leave."

"So he would just come up to you, and tell you to get a girl in the room?" Her voice is as soft, and low as mine is. I can tell that she is trying to make me feel as comfortable as possible.

"Yes" After I notice that she is really paying attention my voice gets stronger as I'm gaining more confidence.

"How did you get them to go?" Now, it's starts to bother me how closely she is paying attention.

"Am I in trouble?" I like Ms. Greer I don't want her to be mad at me.

"No Connie you are not in trouble. You are a child. Children are taught that they are supposed to do what grown- ups tell them."

"I didn't know that somebody would get hurt. I mean I never wanted that." I want to get out how I feel right in the beginning.

"Connie I know. Now tell me. How did you get them to go?"

"Some of them got money, but all of us got to stay up late on Friday and Saturday. We also got things the other kids didn't. Like pizza, McDonalds and Ice cream." When she reaches across the table to grab my hand. I know it's about to get hard.

"Connie tell me about Amy?" I knew it. I didn't want to talk about Amy.

"Well, when she came she use to cry all the time. Always wanted her mommy.

'Cept I heard a pimp killed her mommy. What's a pimp? Anyway, somebody killed her too, so I guess now she is with her mommy.

"I already know all that, but how did she get in the room? Did Mr. Townsend tell you to get her in there? Tell me what happened." Her voice is as soft as I have ever heard a grown-up talk.

"Well white kids didn't usually come to the juvenile home. At least none did while I was there except Amy. Amy had only been there a few days before Mr.Townsend told me to get her to the room. I told him she was too little, but he wouldn't listen. They were already doing it to the boys, so for them it was no big deal .Amy was just too little. Plus, she didn't care about no extra stuff. All she wanted was her mommy, so that's what I told her. I told her to wait in that little room, and somebody would take her to her mommy. She was in there a long time 'cause soon it was bedtime and I went to bed. Then Angie woke me up screaming. Talking about Amy was in that room with no clothes on and she was dead." The longer that my story was the more my voice would get stronger. "I ran in the hallway to see what is going on, and that's when Mr.Townsend comes to me telling me I have to leave. I ask him what happened to Amy, and he says that he didn't know, but that I should run down the stairs and climb out the window and run away.

I told him that I am just a kid, and didn't know where to go. Then he tells me to wait for him by the garbage cans, and I did. That's when the police found me." After I finally get it all out it is almost like a relief. I blow out my breath and sit back in my chair.

"Wow that was some adventure you had, but tell me this. When your room was searched they found over 2,000.00 in it. Where did you get all that money?"

"See Mr.Townsend paid me like 10 dollars every time I got somebody in the room." I bring my voice back to a whisper.

"You know what Connie? Just don't worry about this right now. Soon you will have to tell a judge everything that you just told me. Do you think you can do that?" I raise my head to let her know that I am not afraid.

"Yes" I make sure that my voice is strong.

"Good now eat your pancakes, so that I can take you back." I stop with the fork half-way to my mouth.

"Ms. Greer I don't want to go back there. Isn't there somewhere else I can go?" I can tell that she understands that I don't want to go back there.

"Well your grandparents have said that they were willing to take you in. Would you like to go there?" I almost jump out of my seat.

"Yes. Oh please. Anything would be better than going back to Grandma Mabel's house."

"Okay, well hurry up, and eat your pancakes we have a long drive ahead of us."

All during our drive I keep imagining what life has in store for me. Something good has to happen to me sometime didn't it?

\* \* \*

"Well Connie we're here. Remember to behave yourself, and do what your grandparents tell you to do. I think that from now on you are going to have a good life."

I sure hope so. I follow Ms.Greer to the door, and wait while she rings the bell.

"Good morning... Ma dear. Little Connie is here."

I could hear my grandmother rushing to the door. She snatches the door open, and the first thing that she says is,

"Oh goodness. Look at you. You're down right filthy. Come right on in, and go straight to the bathroom so you can have a bath."

I didn't know whether to be embarrassed or happy. I do know one thing that bathtub sure did sound good.

As I am sitting in the bathtub my grandmother starts to talk.

"Connie we know that you have been through a lot, and that's why when God told me in my dream that I had to let you come live here with us, so we could give you a good life like we gave your father I told your grandfather right away. Now, you know that it's very important to follow all of Gods laws so our only rules here are that you follow the ways of God. Do you understand that?" I stop playing with the bubbles long enough to give her my un-divided attention.

"Yes ma'am I know that I have to go to church. It's okay I like church." I start back playing in the water.

"Well that's good, 'cause there is something going on at the church every day and since your poppa is the pastor. We must be there."

"Every day? You mean I have to go to church every day?"

"Yes. Plus, it's very important that every day you read your Bible and pray. You have seen too much in your young life, and you need the Lord to make you clean.

You will be 12 years old next week. That means you will be responsible for your own sins and you have got to be ready."

I thought about this for a while, and decide I will give it a shot. Maybe things are starting to get better for me.

## Chapter 5

"I sing because I'm happyyy and I sing because I am freeee. His eyes are on the sparrow and I know He watches... me." I open my eyes and people are crying and shouting, standing up and clapping. I look out in the audience and my grandmother is sitting right in the front row. Just nodding her head and fanning herself. My granddaddy starts to speak into his microphone and I know that's my cue to go sit down.

"Brothers and sisters let's all bow our heads in prayer."

I try to concentrate. I really do, but all I can think about is those greens grandma cooked this morning. I have been with my grandparents for a whole year. I have gained 100lbs. Now, along with being black jokes. I got fat jokes. Black as the ace of spades, but big as the whole deck. They say that I was black as an African, and must have found all the food they didn't get. It was hard on me as I was in the 8th grade and it was my last year in junior high school. Being the black, fat preachers' kid is just plain awful.

All the girls my age are really starting to like boys that year. And the boys are already crazy over girls. My grandmother told me she is having none of that foolishness in her house, and besides my grandfather would kill me. My grandfather thought just because I could sing, and remember scriptures I had a calling from God, and was heading towards the ministry and it was his personal job to make sure I get there. He didn't understand about school, and kids and how they could make you feel. Easter was coming up and I was very nervous. For my Easter speech I have to recite all of third John of the Bible. It is 1 whole chapter of scripture. I am so scared of messing up all I did is practice it, and read it over and over. I even forgot all about my schoolwork.

* * *

One morning our algebra teacher tell us we are getting ready to take a test. To turn in all the worksheets we have been given last week, and clear our desks.

I start sweating when he gets to me. I tell him I didn't have my homework somebody yells out,

"Maybe she ate it."
Somebody else yells out,

"Maybe some of that black rubbed off on it."

The teacher just looks at me then he says,

"Connie, where is your homework?"

I have had it. I just put down my head and cry.

"Boo-hoo listen to the whale blubber"

All the kids laugh at me except this one girl Trudy. She is the prettiest girl in the 8th grade. She is very light skinned, and she has light brown eyes, and long hair. "Mr.Murphy here it is right here. She must have dropped it. "Don't cry Connie I found it. It's right here."

I raise my head and look back. She has the prettiest smile.(even if she did have braces. I thought they were cute)

"See Connie, Trudy has your homework. There is no need to cry. Since you are so upset right now you can take your test tomorrow. You just settle down now."

The rest of the period flies by. I just sit and look at Trudy. I can't believe that she had helped me.

"Come on Connie let's walk to choir together." Trudy holds her arm out to me.

"You really want to walk down the hall with me?" She looks at me like I am absolutely crazy.

"Of course silly. Why not?" After I say this she really looks at me like I am crazy.

"How do you know my name?" Sometimes the silliest things come out of my mouth. Now I bet she is already regretting talking to me. She pulls me to my feet.

"Girl we go to your church, plus we are in almost all our classes together." Her hand slides down to my hand and off we go down the hall together.

"How come you never talked to me before?

And I never see you at church." People are stopping to stare all the while.

"That's probably because you sit on the front row, but I see you and hear you. Man you can sing good. Why don't you ever sing solos here at school?" She stops and places her hands on her slim hips.

"Why? So everybody can call me names and laugh at me? No thanks." I begin to walk off without her. She runs to catch up.

"I'll bet if they heard you sing they wouldn't be laughing no more." She links arms with me again, and we continue talking and whispering all the way to our next class.

"Trudy, what are you doing with her?" Trudy stops talking mid-sentence. Frowning up her face because the girl had the nerve to interrupt her while we are talking.

"This is Connie, and she is gonna be my best friend."

I couldn't believe my ears. I am going to be Trudy's' best friend? Everybody in the choir room is laughing.

"Yeah, we know her. You can't miss her." This smart mouth class clown yells from the back of the room.

"Well, she can lose weight, but you're still gonna be ugly." She starts wiggling her head around on her shoulders like the girls from the projects do. "Yeah, and she still gonna be black. Ha-Ha."

I start inching away from Trudy. I didn't want trouble for her because of me.

"Connie where are you going. We're not scared of them."

She takes off her earrings, and everything. She is going to fight to protect me. Nobody has ever protected me before.

"No Trudy we ain't gonna fight them. It won't help. They still gonna talk. Just ignore them. That's what I been doing." I place my hands on her arms to stop her from going over there where they are.

"Well I know what will shut them up. Come on. Mrs. Rogers. Connie wants to sing the solo part." She pulls me up toward the piano where Mrs. Rogers is warming up.

"Why I didn't even know that Connie could sing. Connie do you want to sing the solo? Cause if you do you will have to audition in front of the whole class." I think maybe she thought that would scare me.

"That's okay. She sings in front of the whole church every Sunday." Trudy is a cheerleader, and right now she sounds like my personal one.

"Well then Connie come here."

I am stuck I can't say that I am nervous. I sing in front of hundreds of people all the time. Just never in front of a bunch of kids.

"Come on times a wasting."

I walk down close to the piano.

"Okay. Do you know the solo part to the song, or do you need the words?" She looks up at me while her hands are fumbling through the stack of papers on her desk.

"No ma'am I know it." I look up as she starts to play, and everybody is staring at me. Trudy is smiling and nodding her head.

"Baby look at me, and tell me what you see. You ain't seen the best of me yet look in my eyes, and I'll make forget the rest. I got more in me than baby what you see. I can catch the moon in my hands don't you know who I am? Remember my name."

The choir is supposed to come in there, but everybody just stands there with their mouths open. Trudy and Mrs. Rogers are clapping.

"Very, very good Connie. My. My. I had no idea you could sing like that. Of course you may have the solo part."

I started looking around and people were looking at me different. Some were even smiling a little.

"Well I'll be. If I knew this I would have sang a long time ago. Trudy is so smart. We practiced the song the rest of the class. The kids really began to warm up to me.

After class some are even coming up to me to tell me how good I sound.

"I told you we would shut them up. See didn't I? Come on, so we can get a good seat on the bus. I've got to tell you something."

She is acting like we have been friends forever.

"Do you want to come over my house for a little while? I can help you study for your test tomorrow. Since I already took it, I know what's going to be on it.

"No I've got to work on my Easter speech. I'm doing 3$^{rd}$ John" We sit down in our seat on the bus.

"The 3$^{rd}$ John in the Bible? All of it?" She looks like she is shocked, but I'm used to it.

"Yeah it's only 1 chapter, but it's hard." She flops back into her seat.

"Man being a preachers' kid must be awful." She has a look of total pity on her face.

"Yeah, everybody expects you to be perfect. Especially the preacher." She is nodding her head in understanding.

"Well, I don't expect you to be perfect. I like you just the way you are." I get this bid Kool-Aid grin on my face.

"Why do you like me?

You can probably get anyone to be your best friend. You're the prettiest girl in school." I know that she can see the look of doubt on my face.

"Yeah, I guess it's just that everybody expects me to be perfect all the time. I figure you felt the same way I did, so everyone else would think we are perfect, but together we can really be ourselves. Isn't that a good idea? Plus, I really want to get to know you. Everybody teases you all the time, but you just walk around like you don't have a care in the world. You don't care what anybody thinks." Something on her fingers must be pretty important, cause she is really interested in them all of a sudden.

"That's because what they say about me is true. I am fat, and I am black .What else can they say? They don't know me. Trust me there are worse things they could say."

"I wish I was like you. I have to be very careful everyday about what clothes, and shoes to wear. I have to keep my hair, and make-up done. They watch everything about me. I can't even have the boyfriend I want." She jerks back as the bus jerks to a stop.

"Everybody knows you go with Tyler Banks he is the finest boy in school. Don't you want him?"

"Girl no. I want Terry Phillips." I screw my face up like I have been sucking on sour lemons all day.

"Girl he blacker than me. Why would you want him?" She gets this dreamy look in her eye.

"I like his chocolate skin. Plus he is the star basketball player and he is always looking at me."

"That's cause you are beautiful. I'm always looking at you too, but that doesn't mean I want to be your girlfriend." We grab each others hands and proceed to walk down the street.

"Connie you are so crazy. I am so glad that we are friends."

## Chapter 6

Easter Sunday church is packed. People I have never seen before are there acting like they come every week. I have a new song to sing, and I am kind of nervous, but Trudy is sitting right on the front row with me.

"Calm down Connie. You sing every week. You will be just great, and I'm gonna be sitting right here. Now what you better be nervous about is that Easter speech. Did you get those last 2 verses down last night? Girl yo' granddaddy will kill you if you mess up." She is reaching up to fix the bow in my hair.

"I know, I know I got it down. I wish I didn't have to come to church on Easter. Look at all these people." Now I begin to straighten my dress.

"Girl I know what you mean Easter and Christmas is always like this." With that said she sits down, and pushes me toward the front.

"There goes the choir you better get up there. Just close your eyes, and let the spirit move you."

"I will. Just pray for me girl okay?" I look back like I am walking to the executioners 'chair.

"Always."

*  *  *

"Man I'm glad that's all of church today. We have been there all day long." I plop down, and pull off my shoes.

"Quit complaining you must admit we did have some fun. That song you and Deacon Ed sang was so beautiful." She sits down right next to me. She doesn't plop though.

"Yeah, but girl then the whole choir was gone." I place my feet in her lap so that she can rub them for me.

"Yeah I think I even got the Holy Ghost today." Now that is really funny.

"Oh Trudy. I am so glad that you are my friend. "I feel so good. I never knew that having a best friend could be so special.

"Connie I'm glad that you are my friend too. Who would I tell all my secrets to?" I look at her then like she is totally off her rocker.

"I'm sure you would have found someone." I shake my head at that girl. She can be so silly.

"Well I have a really big secret to tell you."

"What now? You bought some new shoes?" I have no idea what is going through that crazy girls mind.

"No silly. I want you to tell Terry Phillips that I like him." I sit up straight then. "Nunt-un I ain't. What about Tyler?" I turn around and look at her so that she could see how serious I am.

"Who cares about him? He thinks he's prettier than I am." She cracks up.

"I think he is too." Now I start laughing.

"Oh Connie I'm serious. Please." I pull her hand off my arm.

"He's a bad boy Trudy. They say he has even been suspended from school for fighting." I grab her hand to make sure that she continues looking at me.

"I don't care. I want him." Now she plops back pouting with her bottom lip poked out.

"Okay, if you really want me to. I will, but when this blows up in your face I'm telling you right now I'm going to say I told you so." She is so excited about my agreeing that she jumps off the couch , and starts jumping up, and down. We go off down the hall to my room.

"Alright,alright go to sleep. We have a big day tomorrow."

\* \* \*

"Okay there he is on the bleachers. Connie remember don't be afraid. He's only a boy, and he won't bite." She pushes me in his general direction. "Don't worry Trudy. I'm not afraid. I'll be right back." I walk up to Terry ,and his friends goofing off.

"Hi Terry." All the boys just stop joking around and look at me like I'm retarded for coming up to them.

"What's up?" He turns toward me.

"Can I talk to you for a minute?" He crosses his arms across his chest.

"Come on Terry. What chu doing talking to that blimp anyway?" His friends try to pull him away.

"Y'all chill out. She cool. What do you want Connie? I gotta go." I'm really glad that he put them in their place.

"Well...Trudy told me to tell you that she thinks you are cute and she likes you." His whole face lights up when he hears what I have to say.

"Word? Give me her phone number and I'll call her later." It's my turn to look stupid now.

"Her step-dad doesn't like boys to call her, why don't you give me your number so she can call you?"

"Alright bet. You got a pencil and paper in your purse?" I start to dig down into my purse. "Yeah. I think I do. Here it is. What is the number?"I'm trying to write his name on the paper fast, so that she will know who this number belongs to.

"555-1274 she can call me anytime." He winks at me, and turns and walks away.

"Okay. Thanks see you later." He stops walking right in his tracks before he turns back to speak to me.

"Naw thank you."   I run back over to where Trudy is waiting for me.

"Trudy. Trudy. I got his number. He said you can call anytime." She starts jumping up and down like a little kid she is so excited.

"Aaah. Tell me every word he said." I start walking away, but reach back and grab her arm to pull her along with me.

"I just did. Let's go." She begins chattering like a mag pie.

"Do you think he likes me?" I abruptly stop walking to look at her.

"Of course he does, when I thanked him for the number he said ,naw, thank you." She snatches my arm back toward her.

"You didn't tell me he said that. I thought you told me everything he said?"

"Well, now I did." I begin walking once more.

"Oh girl when do you think I should call him? Should I wait a few days, and play hard to get, or call him today?" She stops me again. At this rate we will never get to where we are going. "Well playing hard to get is out since you made the first move. I would call him tonight." Sometimes to be so beautiful Trudy can be pretty stupid.

"What am I going to say to him? I've never talked to a boy that I really like before. What if I say something stupid?" I almost tell her that she already has, but I don't.

"You won't. You know how to talk to people."

* * *

For the next 2 months Trudy and Terry talk on the phone all the time. I am so jealous. She would be on the phone at her house, and even when she would be at my house she would be on the phone talking to that dumb boy. One day she told me that Terry was coming over her house. She said her mom and step-dad would be at work. She wanted me to be there with her.

"Trudy, if we get caught we are gonna be in so much trouble. Why does he want to come over anyway? Yall talk on the phone all the time, and see each other at school."

"Girl he wants to do it to me, and I said yes." She pulls me close to her, and whispers.

"What? Are you crazy? Don't do that." I have got to make her see how dumb this really is.

"Yes I am, and he is going to bring someone for you too." When she says this she says it like she is doing me a favor. "No, now wait a minute, do you think I'm gonna do it too?" I really look at her like she is crazy.

"Yes Connie Of course I do. We are best friends, and should lose our virginity together." My mouth flies open.

"But I don't even know that boy that Terry is bringing over here for me. What if I don't like him? What if he doesn't like me?" I'm so nervous all of a sudden.

"Don't be silly. It won't matter if you don't like him. You're doing this for me. And all boys are nasty, and will do it to anybody. Don't worry I told Terry to pick one of his nice friends, and to make sure that he is light skinned. See how I look out for you?

I knew that you wouldn't want anyone who was dark." She's standing there like she is really proud of herself. "That's true but at least you're in love with who you are doing it to. You want me to do it to a total stranger. And what if we get caught? My grandfather will have a stroke right on the spot.

"Don't worry. We won't. I have it all planned out. As soon as my parents leave I'm going to call Terry. They are going to come right over. We are going to do it then they are going to leave." She acts like she is dusting her hands off.

"Trudy are you sure about this? Do you really know how to do it anyway? What if it hurts?" I know that it's going to to hurt. I wonder if she does.

"Terry told me all about it. He said that it will only hurt for a little while in the beginning. Then it will feel good. All you have to do is take off your pants and panties, and lay down, open your legs. They will stick their thing in and hump us for a little while and that's it."

I didn't want to tell Trudy that I know all about it. Cause maybe then she wouldn't want to be best friends anymore. No way. I'm keeping my mouth closed. She will find out that there is much more to it than she thinks on her own.

"Okay Trudy. I'm gonna do this, but only because you are my best friend." Yeah. I'm gonna let her think whatever she wants.

"Yeh. I knew you would do it. Terry said that you wouldn't go through with it." She wraps her arms around my neck in complete abandon.

"Yeah well Terry is wrong. He must never have had a best friend who he'd do anything for huh?" I hug her right back.

"You'd do anything for me? That's sweet. Cause I'd do anything for you to." She actually kisses me.

"Yeah,yeah. When is this supposed to happen anyway?" I'm starting to get nervous now.

"Saturday. Don't worry. It will be fine." She looks scared to death.

"Connie, I am so nervous. Does my hair look alright?" I smile gently at her trying to reassure her.

\* \* \*

"Yes you look gorgeous as usual, but what about me? Do I look alright?" She is fixing her clothes and everything. I don't have the heart to tell her that he is not going to care one bit about her clothes.

"Yes you are absolutely beautiful." I place both my hands on her face.

"Now I probably wouldn't say all that. Never the less here they come."

(Knock, knock, knock)

"Hey Terry. I thought you'd never get here." I move out the way so that they could walk through the door.

"Oh we left as soon as you called. Hey Connie. this my boy Eric. Eric this is Trudy's best friend Connie." He looks like he is mad as a mug.

"Hey what's up?" He gets right to the point.

"So we gon' do this or what?" Terry directs the question at Trudy.

"Yeah come on up here. I made a big palate on the floor in my room." He stops walking all of a sudden.

"Both of us gon do it in this spot?" He looks at the palate in disbelief.

"Yeah, me and Connie already tried it out we have enough room." He just shrugs his shoulders

"Okay let's get it on." I have to speak up.

"I hope yall got some rubbers or no deal." I want them to know I am serious about this.

"Fo sho, fo sho"

Me and Trudy took off our pants and panties and lay down. Terry couldn't take his eyes off Trudy, but Eric is looking at Terry like he wants to kill him .After a little while he shrugs his shoulders and begins to unbuckle his belt. I look over at Trudy and see her buck her eyes when she sees Terry's thing.

"Uh Terry you can't put that thing in me. It won't fit." Her voice shakes a little. "Yes it will. Now y'all don't forget it's gonna hurt a little bit at first, but then it gone feel real good."

They got down on the floor between our legs, and Trudy closes her eyes tight while reaching for my hand. I grab her hand, and feel Erics' thing go in.

It didn't hurt. It burns a little, but that's all. It is over in about 5 minutes.

"Connie you alright? I wasn't trying to hurt you." Eric gets up to fix his pants.

"Eric I'm fine thanks for asking." I sit up and look over at Trudy.

"Baby you okay? Did it feel good to you?" I can tell that she is not going to tell the truth. I am so worried about her now.

"Yeah Terry it felt good after a minute." She forces a smile on her face.

"See I told you it would. You want us to leave now, or can we stay for a while?" He looks back and forth between Trudy and myself.

"Y'all better go. I don't want to get caught." They are running out the door before I can finish talking.

"Okay." The door slams behind them.

"Bye Connie uh... thanks" I don't even know what to say.

"Bye Eric nice meeting you" I guess he figures it out now.

"Oh yeah. Me too" (Trudy pushes them down the stairs and out the door.)

"Thank you Connie. I know that was just awful. I won't ever ask you to do that ever again, but I'm glad that our first time was together."

I couldn't tell Trudy it wasn't my first time. My first time was long ago, but I was glad that I was there for her. And I would do it again if she asked. What were best friends for?

## Chapter 7

I start to see less and less of Trudy. She is always someplace with Terry. I know that she is telling her mom that she is at my place cause sometimes her mom would call for her to bring something home with her from the store, or something. I told her this too. So she gives me Terrys' number to call her when that happened. I am starting to really worry about her. Plus, I miss her. She has stopped going to school, and everything. I just know something bad is going to happen to her, and sure enough one day something does.

* * *

"Connie I need you to meet me at McDonalds downtown right now. It's very, very important. I really need you. You are still my best friend aren't you?" I switch hands on the phone.

"Yes Trudy I'm still your best friend, and I'll be there as soon as I can." I wonder what is wrong, but figure I would find out soon enough.

"Don't sit down. Go order something to eat. Wouldn't you think it strange to see a fat girl in McDonalds with no food?" She's right. So I walk back up to the counter.

"Okay, I'll be right back. That comment hurt my feelings a little bit, but she was right. I'll have a number 1 with coke and no ice and a cherry pie." As I was going back I thought I could have left the pie, but since I was ordering I might as well go all out.

"What's wrong Trudy?" As I sit down I can tell that something is seriously wrong.

"Oh Connie it's just awful. I'm 8 weeks pregnant."

I drop a handful of fries I am just about to shove into my mouth. "You're what?" I couldn't believe that I heard her correctly.

"You heard me. I'm pregnant." I sadly start to shake my head.

"Trudy. You're only 14 years old. You can't be nobody's' mama. What were you thinking?" She drops her head and whispers.

"I know. You're right, and that's just it. I wasn't thinking." She starts playing with the food on her tray.

"Have you told Terry yet?" She slowly shakes her head.

"Yeah, he says no sweat. Just have an abortion, but you know that I can't do that." I feel so sorry for her.

"So what are you going to do? You have to tell your mama, and she is gonna tell your step-father who is going to kill you." She begins to cry.

"Connie I'm so scared" Her voice drops to a whisper.

"Girl wasn't yall using rubbers?" She hugs herself.

"Sometimes, but Terry said he couldn't feel it right with a rubber on." I roll my eyes.

"Oh yeah sure he couldn't. Now I guess he can feel this" I couldn't believe what she says next. "He broke up with me. Said I was trying to ruin his chances of going to the NBA." Now I want to kick his butt.

"No that black, nappy- head boy didn't." I slam my hand on the table.

"Yes he did." I get up without ever touching my food.

"Well come on we might as well tell your mama and get this over with." I pull her up next to me.

"You mean you'll go with me?" She looks shocked.

"Of course I will...."

"I know, I know what are best friends for. Come on."

\* \* \*

"You are what? Girl have you lost your mind? What in the world are you going to do with a baby? When did you start having sex? Who is the boy? Where does he live?" Trudy drops her head. Tears start rolling down her face.

"Mama he broke up with me. He said I am trying to mess up his life." She tries to make her mama feel sorry for her.

"Well I guess he doesn't think getting you pregnant messes up yours. You go up to your room. Wait till your father comes home. And take Connie with you. Connie I hope you are not doing this shameless stuff with her. Your poor grandfather would lie down and die." I see that they notice me for the first time.

\* \* \*

"Girl what are you doing? Your step-father will be here any minute." She throws stuff into a duffle bag.

"I'm packing my stuff. I'm leaving here." She is just pacing back and forth.

"But where are you going to go?"

"To Terrys' house where else. It's his problem too. We are just going to have to deal with it." I try to stop her from talking.

"Trudy you are only 14. You need your mama. Who is going to help you?"

"Why Connie you are. Aren't you the one always saying that's what best friends are for?"

"Yeah Trudy, but this is too much."

"Why, 'cause it's hard and scary? Well if you only want to be my friend when things are good then I don't need you. I maybe made a mistake when choosing my best friend. Just go on back home. I don't need you."

"Please Trudy don't say that. Of course I will help you. We will do this together. You didn't make a mistake when choosing your best friend. I am your best friend, and will always be there no matter how hard it gets."

Oh God please don't let Trudy stop loving me. She is the only friend I've ever had. I wrap my arms around her neck, and we are hugging when I notice her step-father standing in the doorway.

"Your mama telling me that you're pregnant. Is that true girl? Answer me? She says she wants you to get an abortion. I say Ima beat that baby right outta you. Do you hear me girl?"

I can't move. I'm stuck watching things happen just like watching a movie. Trudy reaches down into her bag, and pulls out a gun. Turns around, and starts pulling the trigger. She shoots her step-father more times than she could count. I hear her mother screaming and running up the stairs, and I know that I have to do something. I run over to Trudy, and grab the gun away from her. By this time Trudys' mom is standing in the doorway with her hand over her mouth.

"No Connie. What have you done?"

I look up and Trudys' mom is just screaming at me. It takes a minute, but then it dawns on me. She thinks that I have shot her husband. I look over at Trudy, and she has tears streaming down her face. She looks at me and begins to open her mouth. I shake my head no. Telling her to be quiet. I don't know where Trudy got the gun from, or even why she has it. I just know that I can't let her do this on her own. I love her too much, and besides that's what best friends do.

Trudy's mom calls the police and everybody starts asking questions. I put my finger to my lips telling Trudy to not say anything. They take me and Trudy to the juvenile home. We only stay 1 night. The next morning we go to court. My grandparents are there, and half the church. The judge says that there will be no trial. He is ruling the shooting an accident, but because Trudy's step-father died. We are both being sent to Louis B. Johnsons Training Home for girls until we are 18 since neither of us will tell what happened. I remember the caseworker telling us he is putting us on the drive 55 system. It is the first chance we have had to talk.

"Connie I don't know what to say about what you did for me. You could still be back at your grandfathers' church singing your heart out."

"Is that what you think made me happy singing? If that was the case I would've been happy long ago because I've been singing since I can remember."

"You make me happy Trudy. Your love and your friendship. Nobody has ever cared about me before. Don't you see? If I had lost you I would have died right on that floor with your step-dad. We will be okay. As long as we stick together we will always be okay."

"If you say so Connie, but I'm scared, and what about my baby?"

"Your mom will change her mind and come pick it up you'll see."

"Alright girls this is your new home so behave yourselves."

All I can see behind the small house is a large fence. Inside that fence back off a ways are little buildings. I can see lines of kids walking around, and think to myself Trudy what in the world have you gotten us into? Come on Trudy let's go on in. It won't be so bad. At least we will be together

"Connie this is the first time I've been away from home. How am I supposed to deal with this?" Trudy is wringing out her fingers, and stepping from one foot to the other I can tell that she is so nervous.

"You just do. You know why? You don't have any other choice." After I say that she stands up a little straighter.

"Let me explain how things work here. We use something called positive peer culture. You will be in a group of 10. Your group will do everything together. The two of you will be assigned to the same group, but from this moment on you will not be allowed one on one conversation. You must always have a third person for talking. You will sit down with house staff every afternoon. During this time you will discuss infractions of the rules. You must always be aware of your group members. If you see doing something wrong you must check them. If they continue the behavior you ask them if they see themselves showing a problem. We encourage all of our girls to confront and work on their problems. You will have a staff member as a group leader and will meet with him weekly. You will also be expected to attend school. You will have a staff member as a group leader and will meet with him weekly. You will also be expected to attend school, you will have little leisure time, but what time you do have will be spent doing something constructive. Do you ladies understand this?" Even though it was too much to grasp we both nodded our heads.

"Very well allow me to escort you to your group members."

As we walk pass groups of girls I notice none turn to look at us. They keep their eyes straight ahead. We get to a cottage in the back and walk inside. In what looks like a big living room a group of girls are sitting on the furniture all watching this beautiful very tall, pretty girl.

"What chall looking at? Yeah, Mr. Brown. It's Libby again showing her tail. Who you done brought in here now? I hope they gon' be in our group, cause as yall can see I really need some help." She stands there popping her gum like there is no tomorrow. "As a matter fact

Libby yes, they are gonna be in your group. Are you going to show them around the cottage?" Her eyes buck in surprise.

"What? You want me to be a tour guide? Sure why not. What's yall name?" She turns to look at us with her left hip stuck out, and her hand propped on it.

"My name is Connie, and this is Trudy." I point to myself, then Trudy. When I introduce Trudy she curls up her lip.

"Trudy can't talk for herself?" I push Trudy behind me.

"Don't worry about what she can do for herself as long as I'm around." I point my finger in the center of her chest.

"Okay, okay chill big girl. Is that cho girl? Hey Natalie. We got another one here. Ha-Ha." She turns and yells at this little boy looking girl.

"Look we ain't like that. That's my best friend, and she is pregnant so lay off."

## Chapter 8

"Oh Connie I don't feel so good." Trudy grabs hold of my arm and bends over at the waist.

"Check yourselves. Yall know yall need thirds to talk." Libby glares at us. "I don't care about that. My back hurts, and my stomach hurts." Libby gets a concerned look on his face.

"Trudy please sit down. I'll go get some help. Mr. Garcia. Mr. Garcia. Trudy doesn't feel good." Mr. Garcia runs out of the office.

"Aren't you 9 months pregnant now?" As Trudy lays back on the couch she says,

"Yes. Please help me. Please." The look that is on her face shows that she is in a great deal of pain.

"Oh shoot. You probably finna have that baby. I knew you was gon have it on my shift. Let's get you to the infirmary." He gently grabs her arm and pulls her up from the couch.

"Can I go with her?" Mr. Garcia stops me as I approach them.

"No Connie. She is probably going to the hospital, and you can't go." I try to get to her anyway.

"But she needs me. Who is gonna help her?" I raise my arms in mock defeat.

"Can't nobody help that girl, but God now. She gon have to do this all by herself." Libby slouches down in the arm chair across the room.

"Libby how you know so much about it?"

"Cause I had two kids. What chall looking at? Hoes can't have kids?"

"Libby where are your two kids now?"

"Well 1 is wit my mama. She can't afford to get the 2$^{nd}$ one, so I had to leave it at the hospital."

"Oh no. How could you do that? My mama is gonna come get my baby. Right Connie?"

"That's right Trudy you just go with Mr. Garcia. Everything is gonna be just fine." She turns to look at me with this really sad face.

"You better hope so. Cause you think that girl coo-coo now. If she has to leave that baby she really gonna be messed up. Man I had to get high for 3 days and nights to deal with that." I wanted to smack her face. I am so sick of her being do negative all the time.

"Trudy is gonna be just fine. I just know it. Ain't no way her mama gonna be able to resist that little baby." I look down at the floor cause I really wasn't sure, but I sure hoped so.

"Girl I hope so. I really do." Then she got up, and walked away.

* * *

"Trudy. You back. I thought you wasn't gonna ever get back. What's wrong? Why won't you look at me? We missed you. All of us have been worried sick about you. Even Libby. We went to church and prayed."

"Y'all must didn't pray hard enough." She doesn't even move. Just stands there with her face pointed towards the ground.

"Why you say that Trudy? You're back and you look just fine." I rush over to her ,and grab both of her hands and place them in mine.

"Yeah, but my little girl got left behind. They have been trying to talk to my mother for 5 days, but she keeps saying no. She say she don't care what happen to me or my baby. Connie she loved that fool more than she loved me. My baby is all alone out there and there ain't nothing I can do about it."

I just sat there looking at her. What am I supposed to say? She is right. There is nothing she could do, and there was nothing I could do either.

After Trudy comes back it seems like time slows down. Everything is so depressing. Trudy stopped talking period, and if we let her she would spend all day lying in bed just staring at the walls in her room. I tried everything I knew how to reach her, but nothing worked. "Trudy please talk to us. I'm sorry about the baby. We all are, but there was nothing we could do. I'm sure that they found your baby a good family. I just know that God is watching over her." I am squatting down in front of her.

"Huh, Connie why didn't you say that? You say everything else. Is God watching out for my baby? You know more about God than anybody I know, so please tell me." She finally looks at me with this blank look in her face.

"Trudy don't do this to yourself. I know it's hard, but you've got to forget about that baby, and move on. You have got to think about yourself." I grab her by the shoulders, and try to shake some sense into her.

"Okay Connie if that's what you want me to do. I will." Then she just gets up and walks to her room.

She comes back out with her shower bag and some clean clothes. On her way to the shower room she says,

"Connie you do know that I love you right?" I look up from the table wondering what that is for.

"Of course I know that. Go take your shower and come be my spades partner." After about an hour I wonder what is taking Trudy so long. I sit there and start thinking about what she said to me before she went to take her shower. I wonder why she would tell me that she loved me like that. I wonder why she had that peaceful look on her face. A look that I hadn't seen on her face for a long time. The more I thought about it the more it bothered me.

"Hey can I get thirds. If nobody will come I'll go by myself." I got up and walk to the shower room door. I stand there a minute thinking about how mad Trudy is gonna be at me for checking up on her. I push open the door and there she is hanging from the pipe by the shower.

I start screaming. Everybody runs to see what the matter is. Mr. Garcia knocks me out of the way and runs into the shower room. He holds onto Trudy while yelling at us to go get him some help. I can't move. It is all my fault. It was my job to protect her. Even from herself. I should have seen this coming, but I didn't. I never knew anyone that had killed themselves before. People always say that it is a coward's way out, but I know better. It takes a very strong person to kill themselves. Staff is running in to cut her down. They lay her on the floor and start doing CPR, but I know that it is too late. My Trudy is gone. Who is gonna be my best friend now? What reason did I have for being there now? Slowly I just sit down on the floor and watch them try to bring Trudy back, but it is too late now.

"Connie I want you to get up and go out with your group. There is nothing you can do in here."

"Mr. Garcia please don't make me leave. That's my best friend. I don't want to leave her alone. If I had been with her this never would have happened."

Mr. Garcia calls for my group to come and get me. They come and try to pull me out of the room. "Noooooo what about Trudy. Who's gonna take care of Trudy?" The real question is who is gonna take care of me.

I had gotten used to having someone to tell all my secrets to. It is hard for me to have to go back to being all alone. I didn't like it one bit.

\* \* \*

"Get the heck out of here. I will kill one of yall." I had gotten worse than Libby. This is the second room I have destroyed and my group members are exhausted. They have to hold me down all the time and I am putting my hands on someone else daily. Almost every night they have to stay awake at night with me. All crowded in my room. Everybody is afraid that I will kill myself like Trudy. I have already tried 8 times in the last 4 months. I just can't get over Trudy being gone. After all I had been through in my life for God to just let me have someone like Trudy in my life, and to then just take her away is too much for my mind to take.

We have a new staff  working in our cottage her name is Mrs. McDaniels. She never says anything to me when I would take off all of my clothes in the dayroom, but this one night it is 4:00 in the morning. My group members are holding me pinned down to the ground trying to talk t to me, and I am just screaming at the top of my lungs. Mrs.McDaniels walks in the room.

"Okay guys you can all go to bed now. I'll take over with Connie from here."

"Wench. What are you gonna do to me? I will mess you up." I lung at her and she threw me down to the floor and sat right on top of me.

I buck and kick and wiggle, but I cannot get her off of me. See Mrs.McDaniels is a great big lady, I am stuck.

"What are you doing Connie? You like it on the floor. That's the only place I've seen you since I got here." She is just sitting on top of me relaxing

"Get your big self-off me." I push with all my might.

"Now I'll make a deal with you. You tell me why your group is up with you tonight, and I'll move." I can't believe that she has the nerve to try and talk to me. She must not know who she is messing with.

"Them broads up with me cause they want to be. I didn't do anything." I begin to wiggle all over again. "Come on Connie. Those girls are exhausted. This is the 3$^{rd}$ night this week you have kept them up all night with your bull. What do you want from them?"

"I don't want nothing. I just want to be left alone." Now I add bucking.

"Okay if you really want to be left alone let me tell you what to do. Stop fighting everybody and stop fighting yourself. Nothing you do is ever gonna bring Trudy back." This time my body went absolutely still. "What in the world are you talking about? Stop saying her name. You didn't even know her." I really want to kill her now.

"I know that she was your best friend. That you guys came here together for a murder that I'm sure you didn't even commit."

The tears I have never once shed, not even when I found her hanging finally begin to fall.

"I know that life has been very hard for you, and now you're all alone again and probably very scared."

The more she talks the harder I cry. I am so tired, and so mad. I am even tired of being mad.

"That's alright baby. Let it out. Let it all out."

I never say anything to Mrs. McDaniels. I just cry myself to sleep. I didn't know when the last time I could go to sleep like that.

Chapter 9

I woke up the next day, and took a shower and got dressed. When I lined up for breakfast everybody is just watching me. I guess waiting for me to show out, but I didn't. I just keep my head hanging down.

"Well Connie whatever it is you're gonna do I wish you would start now. Because I am very tired and want to go to bed early tonight."

"I'm not going to do anything Cathy. I feel real bad for all the stuff I put yall through, but I'm done acting bad now. You'll see."

"Yeah right. She'll be in the mop closet drinking Drano before the day is out." Libby pushes everybody out of her way.

"No I won't. I don't want to die anymore." Libby places her hand on her hip, and looks at me doubtfully. "Why the change of heart?"

"Libbey."Everybody yells out at the same time.

"Not like I want to see another one swinging or nothing. I just want to know how she could put all of us through so much hell for the last few months then stop just like that. I mean we all know the reason for her to start. What is the reason for her to stop?"

"Well I guess I just got tired. Is all. Then once I started crying I couldn't stop. All the bad feelings I had came out with those tears. Now yeah, I miss Trudy, but I don't think it's a good idea for me to die with her. Just like it wasn't a good idea for me to come here with her.

I didn't shoot her step-dad. She did. I didn't even know where she got the gun. I just thought as best friends we were supposed to stick together." Libby shakes her head.

"I always knew you was a fool. I just didn't know you was a damn fool." She walks away talking to herself.

"Connie now you're stuck here for almost 3 years for something you didn't do." Cathy comes over to try and hug me.

"I know Cathy, but I've got a lot of problems. Maybe I will get the chance to work on them while I'm here." Mes. McDaniels walks up.

"Yeah Ms. Thang. You also need to worry about how you are gonna pay for destroying all the states property that you destroyed."

"Mrs.McDaniels they are gonna make me pay for all the stuff I broke? I ain't got no money." I can't believe it.

"Well how about we make popcorn balls, Rice Krispy treats, and cookies and sell them to the other girls here. I'm sure that you can make a lot of money doing that."

I love being with Mrs. McDaniels. She is like the mother I never had, and she is always hugging me. I guess she could tell I never had too many hugs. Everybody says they like me.

* *

Mrs. McDaniels says I only need 2 girls to help me, and everybody else needs to go back to working on themselves.

"I know you ain't gonna pick me, but just so you know you can't get herpes from baking cookies" She looks so sad. I didn't even know that she had Herpes.

"Libby that doesn't have nothing to do with it. As a matter of fact I do pick you, and also Natalie." She looks surprised then starts cracking up. Jackie finally speaks up.

"A ho, dyke and a fat girl. Ha-Ha. I can only guess what kind of stuff y'all gon make."

"Oh Jackie you just mad cause I didn't pick you. Don't be jealous. I'll pick you next time." I start to pat her on the back.

"No you won't. I don't want any of that fat or black to rub off on me. You think everybody think you so special. They don't. They just glad that they ain't got to stay up with your big behind every day. You probably gon eat the cookies fast as you make them. Yo Mrs. McDaniels.? You sure it's a good idea to have Connie make snacks? Ha-Ha."

I want to take the chair that I am sitting in, and smash her in the face with it. I don't know why I thought that I could be a regular kid. People are always going to laugh at me, and call me names. Nobody ever cared about me 'cept Trudy, and now she's gone. Mrs. McDaniels is just doing her job. Jackie is right. Everybody is just tired of me acting a fool.

"Yeah it's funny me making snacks isn't it? But I gotta do it, so I'm gonna. And don't worry. I won't ask you to help me. I don't want to rub off on you now do I?" I roll my eyes, and walk away.

"Alright girls. Enough is enough. Connie why don't you and your helpers go on into the kitchen so we can get started."

"Connie I don't know why you let her get to you. She is just jealous you know." When Naralie places her hand on my shoulder. I shake it off.

"Yeah. I know. From now on I am just gonna play the game. Shoot I know how to do that. I just want to get out of there, but to go where. I have no idea." As I'm standing there daydreaming Mrs. McDaniels walks up.

"Um... Connie I've been making some phone calls about you." I almost jump right out of my skin.

"About what? What did I do now? I'm trying to do better you know. "I automatically poke out my lip.

"Yes Connie I can see that you are doing much better. In fact I don't think you belong here at all. That's why I've been making phone calls." Now it is my turn to look surprised.

"Well what's happening? And you know if I leave here I don't have anywhere else to go." She slyly smiles

"I wouldn't be too sure of that if I were you. Your grandparents seem like really nice people. In fact your grandfather tells me that he misses you very much, and that he knew in his spirit that you could not have committed such a crime." I can't believe she just said that.

"So are you saying that I can go back there?"

"Connie that's exactly what I'm saying."

Wow. I never even thought about going back to my grandparents' house. Shoot I never even thought about leaving here. I always thought I'd mess around and kill myself for real somehow or another.

"This sounds pretty good Mrs. McDaniels. It sounds real good. I guess I'd better really work on getting that G.E.D then so I can go to college when I get out." She is ctazy if she thinks that judge is going to let me out.

"That sounds like a real good plan Connie."

I am working hard in school. I didn't know when I am gonna be able to take my G.E.D I just knew that I wanted to be ready.

"Connie I think on Monday you will take the G.E.D I've been helping you work on your geometry, but now I think you're ready." I knock all my papers off my desk. Ms. Temple bends over to pick them up.

"Really Ms. Temple? I don't think my science is that good, and lately social studies have been kicking my butt" She smiles at me.

"Connie you're ready. I think on Monday you're gonna surprise yourself."

I can't wait to get back to the cottage. I have to tell Mrs. McDaniels about taking the test Monday. Plus, I only owe them 220.00 dollars more in property damages. This will be my last weekend selling snacks. If I have to look at 1 more marshmallow I'm going to scream.

"Mrs. McDaniels. Mrs. McDaniels. Guess what. I'm taking my GED Monday." I run into the office without even knocking. "You are? Girl God really is good. You are also going court on Wednesday next week. You are gonna get out of here." I stop moving. I can't speak. I can't breathe. Can this really be?

"Do you really think so? Do you really think they are gonna let me out of here?" I know that I am whispering, but I am afeaid that if I speak to loudly she will take it back.

"Yes Connie I do. I really,really do."

Chapter 10

Walking in granddaddy's' church again feels so weird. It seems like everybody is staring at me. Especially that boy on the drums. I wonder what his problem is? I know I don't know him. Man I wish people would just stop staring.

"Now I wonder if my beautiful granddaughter would bless us with a song."

What? I know he didn't say what I think he said. I haven't sang in 2 years." Amazing Grace........" church that day is just beautiful. That is definitely something that I have definitely missed.

"Oh Connie that song you sang in church today was beautiful. I really missed your voice around here." I stop eating long enough to hear what she has to say. "Thanks grandma. I really did miss your cooking" I can't wait to get my fork back into my plate.

"I can tell. You better slow down on them greens. You gonna make yourself sick." She is smiling even though she is fussing.

"Grandma. You know I start school tomorrow. Are you gonna drive me?" She looks at me like she wants to fuss, but doesn't want me to feel uncomfortable on my first Sunday home.

"Yeah girl, but you better start studying for that driving test. You're going to college now. You need to be driving yourself."

The next few weeks fly by. I am back singing at church, and school is pretty decent. I am catching the bus there now. I still haven't caught on to driving. On my bus ride to school. I notice a group of boys hanging out by Mr. Reds store. I have never seen these boys before. They are wearing real nice clothes, and big gold chains around their neck. They look like the rap stars on TV, and there is this one. He looks like everybody else looks up to him. He is sooo fine. But I know he would never look at me. Nobody looks at me except that ole dumb boy at church who plays the drums.

We have to go to this youth retreat at church. We are gonna be in Detroit, Michigan for 2 days, so we have to stay in a hotel. Our first day there we go to a big beautiful church. Our drill team does some awesome drills, and our youth choir throws down. I sing a solo, then we go to the hotel. We kids share two rooms, and

Pastor Jamie has her own room. In the middle of the night I am woken up by Pastor Jaime.

"Connie, wake up. Follow me into my room."

I do as I am told. When I get to the room she says, "Connie I have been watching you. I think you are so pretty."

Oh boy. Every time I hear that trouble follows.

"Can I kiss you?" Pastor Jaime is a girl what is this? I just hang my head and nod. She starts kissing me then pulls my gown over my head, but what happens next shocks me. She lay back on the bed opens her robe and spreads her legs...

A few hours later I am back in my room laying on the floor thinking about what has happened to me. Everyone I trust hurts me. I just want to go back home.

"Uh-Uh Connie? You sound real good up there. My name is Cedric. I play the drums."

Did that boy think just because I am fat I can't see? I know he plays the drums.

"I live with my grandparents. Mother and Deacon Scott. I was wondering if you wanted to come over for dinner." I am just about to get in trouble for cussing in church when..."

"Why sure Cedric. Connie would love to come over for dinner. Why don't you go tell Mother Scott while I go tell the pastor."

"Yes ma'am. " He takes off almost running he is so excited.

"Grandma. Why did you tell that ole ugly boy that? I don't want to go over their house for dinner." I am pouting just I use to when I first came to live with them.

"Connie you are a college girl now, and need to go on dates. Cept your grandfather would never allow it. But he really likes Cedric and I do too. He is a nice boy and he loves the Lord. I think he would be a perfect suitor for you."

Well grandma is right. My grandfather loved the idea. Grand-daddy figures Deacon Scott will be as strict as he is, and if I have to go on dates. Deacon Scott's house is the perfect place.

* * *

"Uh Cedric. Where are we going? Your house isn't this way."

"I know my grandmother needs some Pet Milk, and Mr. Reds is the only store open over here. It will only take a minute."

As we pull up in Mr. Red's parking lot I see that group of strange boys. They are listening to some loud rap music coming out of this big black truck. When Cedric goes into the store. The driver's side door opens, and Mr. sooo fine steps out.

"What's happening Miss lady? What's your name? My name is Tony. Everybody calls me T." He has his hand out stretched like I am going to shake it.

"Uh-Uh-Uh my name is Connie everybody..." Before I can even finish my sentence Cedric runs out of the store.

"Ey yo. Man get away from my car. We don't want none of your drugs."

Suddenly the loud music stops and everybody is looking at us to see what is gonna happen next. One of T's boys walks up and pulls up his sweater so that we can see that he has a gun.

"I don't care if you got a gun. I ain't scared of yall."

"Hey my man. Be cool. I am just saying hi to the lady. I didn't mean no harm."

"Yeah well the lady is my girlfriend, and she don't need you to say hi to her." Tony shakes his head and starts laughing.

"Cedric will you just shut up, and come on before you get shot." T smiles this beautiful smile showing all snow white teeth as he backs up. Cedric gets in the car mumbling as he pulls off, and I could have sworn I see T wink at me. I know I'm not gonna be able to sleep for a week. All night I dream about his carmel colored skin, hazel eyes, and curly hair. I have never been fascinated by a boy before. Cedric says he's one of the Detroit boys who came here to sell drugs, and nothing but trouble. Maybe he is, but he's still nice to look at. Oh and he smells good too.

\* \* \*

"Hi Connie. I've only seen you come to this store with your little boyfriend. What chu doing here by yourself?"

"I came here from church. I want to get something to eat in between services if it's any of your business." I almost push him out of the way. "Ouch. Don't bite my head off ma. I am just asking. I thought you liked me? Why you gotta be so mean? (He smiles that beautiful smile again.)" He has got some nerve.

"Boy. I don't even know you, so how you gonna think I like you?" He places his hand over his chesr.

"Oh I'm sorry my mistake. I thought church girls are supposed to be nice girls?" He starts laughing.

"We are when we want to be." I roll my eyes as I turn away.

"You don't want to be nice to me ma?" He grabs me by the arm.

"No. And quit calling me ma. I ain't your mama."

\* \* \*

"Shannon do you know anything about them Detroit boys that be hanging out at Mr. Reds store?" I turn away even though I know she can't see me through the phone.

"Connie what do you want to know about them for? Don't you got a boyfriend? Anyway they are way outta your league." I almost hang up.

"Yes I do gotta boyfriend. I'm just asking is all." I wish she was right in front of me some times.

"Well they sell cocaine and heroin. I think the lead one name is T. They real mean. They be shooting people and setting people on fire. My friend Tangie go wit one of them. His name is Jay. He always giving her money and taking her shopping, but he also got her drinking and smoking weed. She don't hardly even come to class anymore." As I'm listening to her talk I slowly shake my head.

"That's sad I wouldn't let no boy stop me from getting my education."

\* \* \*

"Hi Connie, you gon talk to me today? I know you want to. You always are looking at me." He thinks he is really something.

"Boy don't nobody be looking at you, but I do want to talk to you." I walk right up to him.

"Okay what's up" He crosses his arms across his chest.

"Why y'all come all the way here to sell drugs? I mean can't you sell drugs in Detroit?" He nods his head like he is really paying attention to what I am saying.

"Yeah, but there's too much competition. You know anyone else who sells drugs here?" He holds his arms out and turns back and forth.

"No" He did have a point.

"My point exactly. That's all you want to talk to me about? Why I came here to sell drugs?" He runs his tongue across his bottom lip.

"No I want to know why you always looking at me? Why you want me to be nice to you? You know that you can get any girl in town to be nice to you." I have to say everything in one breath so that I can get it all out.

"Yeah, but they won't be as pretty, or sexy as you." I just shake my head. "Whatever boy. You know I ain't hardly pretty or sexy." "You know what Connie? The sad thing is that I think you really believe that." I know this boy is crazy now.

"I do cause it's the plain ole truth." I'm getting mad now.

"Okay. I'll leave that alone for now, but can we be friends please?" I give him a look that says you have completely lost your mind.

"Uh. I guess that won't kill me, or will it?"

Me and Tony become good friends. Everybody at church and in the neighborhood use to talk about it. Only my grandfather and Cedric really hated it. They both said that I was straddling the fence. They said that I needed to stay away from Tony. That he was a demon and would somehow destroy me. They didn't understand. He listened to me. He never put me down or called me names. In fact he always said that I am beautiful. He always says that I look like the girl on the Dark & Lovely perm box. I use to say I wish. Because even though she is black she is pretty, but I know she looks nothing like me.

## Chapter 11

"Come on Connie please? We have been going together 6 months now." Cedric is just plain pitiful.

"So what. Is that all you want? I thought you was saved? You know we supposed to wait till we get married." I sit back in my seat.

"I know, but it's so hard. I want to so bad. Come on baby please? Just let me stick the head in okay? It won't hurt. I promise." He thinks I am a fool.

"No. and I should tell grand-daddy you asking." When

"No please don't do that. He just start letting me drive the church van. I won't ask no more okay?"

What I listen to that lie for? For the next month he begged and begged. Tony thought it was funny. He said he was glad that church guys got blue balls too. Finally one night...

"Please Connie. I just can't take it no more." This one time can't hurt.

"Okay boy, but you better hurry up, and only put the head in. Don't cum in me either."

Neither one of us had the sense to know that we needed a condom. Even if he was only going to stick the head in.

\* \* \*

"Tracy I been throwing up every day for the past month. My stomach has been killing me." Tracey knew what it was right away.

"Connie I know that you and Cedric ain't doing it? Please tell me that." This girl is so stupid. I ain't telling her all my business.

"Why would you think that? Of course we are not doing it. Girl we saved. But this one time I did let him put the head in." I say the last couple of words at a whisper.

"YOU WHAT? Did he have on a rubber?" She sounds so mad.

"No. He didn't come. He just put the head in." I am kind of scared now.

"Girl I know you ain't that stupid. Both my kids come from just sticking the head in."

Tracy took me to Planned Parenthood, and sure enough I am pregnant.

"Girl what am I gonna tell my grandparents? They are gonna kill me." I am sitting in the car wringing my hands.

"Well you better tell Cedrics' retarded behind first. It's his fault too you know." Actually it is both of our faults, but I'm going to get yelled at enough for both of us.

"Yeah, but I know better. I have been around this situation before." I look down at my lap.

"Girl if you talking about Trudy. This ain't the same situation. Cedric ain't gon leave you, and yes your grandparents are going to be mad but they will get over it."  I look up in almost relief.

\* \* \*

"Hey. Hey T. Come here. For a minute." He runs over to see what I want.

"Alright...what's up ma? Why you look like you been crying? Don't make me burn down your grandfathers church." I am almost too embarrassed to say the words.

"I'm pregnant T. I'm so scared. What am I going to do.?" I'm rocking from side to side. I have been awake all night. "Dang ma. I didn't know that you and ole boy was getting down like that. I thought I was going to be the first one." He starts laughing" Please Tony this isn't a time for jokes. What am I going to do?" He straightens up

"You tell your grandparents yet?"

No. I'm scared." I pull on his arm.

"Well check this out. Ima take you to Detroit to this one place. I'll pay for it and everything. Don't worry I got you." I look horrified.

"Tony are you talking about an abortion? I can't have no abortion. You know I'm saved." I look at him like he has lost his mind.

"Yeah your saved behind shouldn't be pregnant either, but you are." I shouldn't have even come to him.

"No I can't do that." I start to walk away.

"Well I guess you better go tell your folks then. You can't hide it forever. You might as well get it over with. What dat square dude say?" I'm almost to embarrassed to tell him that Cedric doesn't even know.

"I haven't told him yet either. I guess I better go home." The look in his eyes tells me that he feels sorry for me. "Well you know I got cho back no matter what chu do." "You know all you got to do is send for me I'm there." I don't think that I have ever been this sad. "I know thanks."

* * *

"Cedric I need to tell you something".

He has this look in his face like I am bothering him. Before I let him touch me he never acted like that. "What can't it wait? I need to get this van back to church." Now I'm really mad he doesn't even look at me. "No. it can't wait. I'm pregnant." Since he wants to play like that. "You what? How? I mean are you sure?" I don't think I have ever seen his eyes git that big." Yes, I'm sure so you as well come in. We need to tell my grandparents. "He slams himself back into his seat. "Aw man I'm only 19 years old. What I'm gonna do with a baby?" I can't believe that he just said that. I wonder what he thinks about the way that I feel. "What are you talking about? I'm only 17, and you're gonna do the same thing I'm gonna do with it. Raise it. Cause I ain't getting no abortion." He is only thinking about himself. Men are all the same. I didn't say I want you to do that. Come on. Let's get this over with." I could hardly breathe. I know they are in the family room watching TV waiting for me to come home like always. "Uh grandma...granddaddy. We have something to tell you. Cedric is standing behind me scared to death. I pull him up beside me. "Um I'm pregnant." My voice drops to almost a whisper when I say this. "What you say? Yall getting married?" I look at my grandfather like he is crazy. "Yeah... I'm sure that is what the two of y'all saved kids come up in my house and tell me at 10:00 at night." He is so mad that I can actually see steam come out of his ears.

"Uh... why yes sir. That's what she said. We're getting married. Isn't that great?" My grandfather just walks out the room. My grandmother just sits there crying softly to herself. "Grandma. Do you hear them? I don't want to get married. Do something." I stamp my foot like I am 2 years old. "Chile it ain't nothing I can do. Looks like yall done done all the doing in da worl'. If yo' grandfather say that yall getting married aint nothing we can do, but try and get this thing over with before you start showing. How many months is you?" She starts wringing her hands and I can tell that she is as afraid of my granddaddy as I am. "Only 1 grandma. " I sit down slowly. I know it is finished now. "Well good we still got time." The next 3 months I wish I could say they crawled by, but they didn't. Now I am Mrs. Cedric Scott. All the ladies at church are so happy. My grandfather is happy too. I guess because I am finally out of his hair. Happily married to a nice Christian boy who will do whatever he told him to do. I am still going to college, and still talk to Tony whenever I can. I guess you can say he is my best friend now.

* * *

"Hey T." I am so happy to see him. I have looked for him everywhere. "Yeah little mama what can I do for you?" I am so happy to see him that I forget to even get mad at him. "Stop calling me that. Where have you been? I missed you?" I guess he can tell that I am really worried. "5-0 got me. Now I got this little bity case." I start pouting like a small child. "Aw man don't tell me you going to jail. What am I going to do when it's time to have this baby?" He starts to reach for me "Listen to you spoiled and selfish. You ain't worried about me being in jail. You worried about yourself." He gets this small smile on his face. I start to smile as well. "Now you know that's not true. I'm worried about both of us." Ha-Ha. Girl you a trip. When you gon' leave that lame, and get down with a winning team?" He stands in front of me and strikes a pose. "Tony stop that. Cedric is my husband, and the father of my baby. You know that I can't leave him."

* * *

When I turned 9 months Tony went to prison. He got 2-5 for possession with intent to deliver. I felt just awful. And I thought I was fat before I got pregnant. Now I am huge. And Cedric let me know every day. "Connie. Are you sure that you need 2 pieces of chicken? You are gaining more weight every day. That can't be all baby. You are gonna have this little bity baby and still be big as a house. "That's not nice Cedric. You don't have to be mean. Man I wish Tony was out.

(Slap.) "Ow. Why did you hit me?" I grab my right cheek. "For mentioning another man in my house. Tony this and Tony that. I'm tired of hearing about Tony. You sure this my baby?" I am so shocked that he has the nerve to ask me that. "I can't believe you asked me that. Of course this is your baby. I never had sex with Tony." The hurt look is all over my face. "Well actually when you got pregnant we weren't having sex either." He pushes mr down on the couch. "I'm calling granddaddy. Then we'll...Uh-oh my water done broke."

* * *

"Come on chile just hol' on. It'll be over soon." Cedric is sitting over in the corner like it's him that is in pain. "I don't know what she hollering for. We been here all night, and she still ain't had that baby." He sits down in the chair in the corner. "Boy you jus' hush up. This girl having a hard nuff time." I throw my head from side to side. "Grandma he don't care. He doesn't even think it's his." All of a sudden all these doctors and nurses come running in the room. They put everybody out except Cedric. They said that they had to take the baby out right away...

*  *  *

I ain't never been this sore in my whole life. "Connie. Connie you woke up finally." He looks so pitiful sitting there. I almost feel sorry for him. "Where is my baby?" My grandmother is all smiles "Oh don't you worry about this little mama I got her right here." A girl. I knew right away that I was gonna name her Keyona Latrice. I knew from then on my life would never be the same. As long as I made sure her life was nothing like mine I knew she would be alright.

## Chapter 12

"You better make that baby shut up before I have to come in there. You hear me Connie? I said make that baby shut up. Can't even watch the game in this house. I thought you were gonna take her to your grandparents house this weekend?" Cedrock fluffs out his pillow behind his head. "I can't. Granddaddy got a bad cold and grandma is scared the baby will get it. Plus I have this black eye and they will want to know what happened."

Cedric started really fighting me after I came home with the baby. For any reason I would get a fist or a foot in the mouth. I didn't want to tell anyone because everybody thought he was perfect. Just because a man doesn't cheat on you and pays the bills doesn't mean that he is perfect. Well add to that he went to church on Sundays and drove the church van....He was a downright saint.

\* \* \*

I start writing Tony in prison cause well...
I need someone to talk to. He even call a couple
times, but since I am never sure when Cedric
will be home I am not to comfortable with that.
Tony tells me that no man should ever hit a
woman, and all I have to do is say the word and
he will make sure Cedric never hit me or
anybody else again. But I think he knows I
would never let him hurt my husband.

* * *

"Connie. Get in here. (slap.) How many
times do I have to tell you not to put the glasses
away wet? (Slap.) We are gonna have more
roaches than people that live in the projects
have(slap.) you never learn. I have to treat you
like a child. (slap.) And why is that baby crying?
What do you do all day when I'm at work (slap.)
sit around and eat? (slap.) Well when I get done
with you, you are gonna know how to act. "He
knocks me down and starts to stomp on my
head. I just scream and holler. I just know that
he is going to kill me this time. I didn't know
why he beat me all the time. He swears that he
loves me, but if this is love I didn't want any
parts of it.

"Grandma. Please let me in. Grandma.
Wake up. Let me in. "Chile what's the matter?
Why you got that baby out in the cold? What

happened to you? Tell mama what's wrong?" I almost throw myself into her arms. "Cedric. Cedric beat me up. I can't take it anymore. He puts his hands on me every day." She looks at me like she thinks I am making it up. "Well what you do to him?" I can't believe that she just asked me that question. "What I do? I didn't do nothing to him. He crazy. He beats me for everything I do. Whether it's good or bad." My face is a mixture of blood and snot. "Now Connie. I know Cedric. Been knowing him since he was a small child. I know he wouldn't just fight you for no good reason. You must be doing something to him. He is a good man. God fearing. He is a good provider. Don't run around with loose women. Now, I'm gonna call him and talk to him. Ain't no sense in bothering your grandfather with this foolishness. I'll talk to Cedric then you and this baby can go on home like you supposed to be.

Grandma calls and talks to Cedric. He cries and apologizes. Saying he is under a lot of pressure at work, and that he never meant to hurt me. That he loves me and his baby and wantes us both to come home. Grandma falls for every lie that comes out of his mouth. He didn't even mention that he is beating on me every day. Sometimes more than once a day. Or the fact that he never goes near Keyona, and complains about her crying constantly. But in the end grandma drives me back home, and tells me to stay there like a good wife should.

* * *

"Connie. You big,black,stupid cow. I'm gonna kill you." I take off running. I know that I have to get my baby, and get out of there. I can hear him in the bathroom running water in the tub. What is he doing? I've got to hurry. He's really mad now. "There you are. Put that baby down. And get in here." He snatches me by the arm and drags me into the bathroom. "I done told you, and told you about putting too much salt in my food. What you want me to be big and fat like you? Get them clothes off." I wonder what he is gonna do to me now. I beg him to please forgive me as I slowly remove my clothes, but that only seems to make him madder. Once I am naked he pushes me backwards into the bathtub. Once I fall in he grabs an extension cord off the counter and starts to beat me with it. I scream louder and louder. I can feel my wet skin ripping open every place he hits me. He must have beaten me for 30 minutes. Until finally someone grabs his arm.

"Ma'am. Are you okay? An ambulance is on the way." I look up. At first I think that it's an angel. That I have died and gone to heaven. "My baby. I've got a baby." I croak out before I slip back down in the water. "Don't worry ma'am. Someone from your church has your baby. Your friend Tracy called after she heard all the noise. She said that she is supposed to take you to choir rehearsal." He softly pats on my arm as he sits me on the toilet seat. "Yes what's going to happen to Cedric?" I can't believe even after all that he had done to me I want to make sure that he is going to be ok. "Well we're gonna keep him in jail tonight. You have to come down and press charges in the morning, or we'll have to let him go. So make sure you come right to see us once you leave the emergency room. Okay?" I put down my head, because I know that I didn't want to go to the emergency room. Okay well I didn't get to leave the emergency room by morning. They admitted me. Cedric had really messed me up this time. I even had a broken arm. My grandmother came to visit me after I had been there for two days.

"Baby. How are you doing? I am taking good care of Keyona. Why didn't you call me?" She couldn't even look at me. "For what? For you to tell me what kind of a saint Cedric is? No thanks. I know first-hand what kind of person he is." I raise my voice just a bit so that she will know how serious I am. "That's yo' husband chile. Menfolk's can have a little bit of a temper when they young, but once they get a little age on dem deys cool off. A good man is hard to find. You can't be just throwing them away cause of one thing." After what I have been through recently I can't believe she says this to me. "Grandma. Cedric beats me, and one day he is going to kill me if I don't get away from him. Now I'm not going back to him this time." I settled back on the hospital bed. "But chile what is you going to do? Your granddaddy ain't gon let you stay at our house when he knows that you got your own. He loves Cedric. I tol' him what he did and your granddaddy said a night in jail surely has cooled him off. He's learned his lesson." Things with the two of them will never change. I slowly shake my head back and forth.

"Grandma that's crazy. These people here at the hospital told me about this program for women like me. They say me and Keyona can live there and everything until I find me somewhere for us to stay." She looks like she can't believe I am actually considering leaving. "What you gon' do about money. Girl you need money to find you somewhere to stay. Cedric say that he promise to never hit you again baby. Please go home." I just continue to shake my head. This time my mind is made up. "I'm sorry grandma I just can't do that. If something happens to me who will raise Keyona? She will probably end up having a worse life than I've had. Unh-uh. I've got to try to make it on my own."

\* \* \*

Keyona and I go into the domestic assault program. We have our own room and there is a big living room all the women share. We all take turns in the kitchen cooking and we all clean up together. I write Tony and tell him what happened. I also give him the number to the phone we use and ask him to call me.

\* \* \*

"Hello may I speak to Connie Scott?" I take a big breath and prepare myself for whatever he has to say. "It's me Tony. Hi." I sank down in the chair by the phone. "Oh man Connie. I have been going crazy worrying about you. Why won't you let me do anything about this?" I put my head down in my hand. "Because that's not the right thing to do." I guess he can tell that I don't want to talk about this, because he changes the subject. "How are you doing? Are you okay? Do you need anything? Do you need some money?" He is asking questions so quickly. "Dang Tony slow down. You act like you really care or something." I start to laugh. "I do care Connie. I love you. Don't you know that by now?" I can't believe that he just says that. "But why are you just telling me this now? I'm married for God's sake. "So. He doesn't treat you right. I finally figure you and Keyona need something better. Even if it is a life with somebody like me." He sounds shy almost. "Oh Tony I'm scared. You're in prison. I'm out here. It's only a matter of time before Cedric finds me." I bang my fist on the desk. "So leave. I get out of here in 3 months. You can go to Detroit for 3 months. Then when I come home you can come back. That nigga ain't crazy. He wouldn't dare mess with you while you are with me." He isn't make any sense. "How would I get to Detroit? Where would I live? How would I live? "Don't worry just tell me where you are and leave the rest up to me."

Tony sends this lady to pick me up that same day. She says that she is his aunt, and that her name is Kim. She says that I am supposed to stay with her until Tony comes to get me in 3 months. There is just something about her that I can't quite put my finger on, but she is always sniffing her nose and looking around. I think we are never gonna get to Detroit. Detroit is not what I expect. I think everybody is gonna be walking around with gold chains and new shoes on. I was wrong. I have never seen so many poor people in my life. Everywhere I look I see abandoned houses. What in the world have I gotten myself into?

* * *

"Hey Connie. Your room is all ready for you. I got you everything I thought you would need for you and the baby. I filled the refrigerator and cabinets with all kinds of stuff." "Ey. Yo' Kim. Y'all better not touch none of her stuff either.

Here is my beeper number. Page me if you need anything, and I mean anything. I'm gon take real good care of you and Lil Tony until Tony get out." Oh. So that's it. Tony told Jay and the rest of his friends that Keyona is his baby. Wait till I talk to him. "Thank you Jay. Are you going to show me around?" I stop unpacking long enough to give him my undivided attention. "Show you around? For what? You ain't gon need to go nowhere. Anything you need I will get it for you." I put my hands on my hips. "So I'm supposed to just stay in this house for 3 months? Are you crazy? I can't do that." I actually stomp my foot. I know then that I have to get out of here. "Well where are you gonna want to go?" Jay looks so uncomfortable. "I don't know. Maybe the store, maybe church." He has to be able to tell that I am not going to stand for this one bit. "I don't know Connie. We gon' have to talk to Tony about it when he calls." He starts shaking his head as he picks up his keys to leave like the conversation is over. "Yeah you darn right we gonna have to talk to Tony. I did not come up here to be kept prisoner." I slam the drawer shut, and pounce down on the sofa.

                        * * *

"See baby I'm just trying to look out for you. Why you mad?" I pull the phone away from my ear while slowly shaking my head. "Tony I will not be locked up like you are for 3 months. I'm trying to get out of one hell, and you putting me in another one." I speak slowly and calmly so that he knows how serious I am. "What do you want to do then Connie? I'm helping you the best way that I know how. I'm locked up. What can you expect from me? Don't you see that I'm doing the best that I can?" I let out a deep breath. I'm going to have to go back home. I don't see any other way. "Tony yes I do and I really appreciate it. I just can't do this. I'm gonna call Cedric to come and get me."

Chapter 13

Cedric came right away. He didn't even ask what I am doing there. For about 2 months things are going pretty good, and just then out of the blue..."I can't find my black tie. (slap.) Cedric. You promised you would not hit me anymore." I grab my face and turn away. "I didn't hit you. I slapped you. You want me to show you the difference?"

I am Cedrics punching bag once again. I think I am getting numb, because it didn't even hurt no more. He would knock me down, and I would get up like he hadn't even done nothing.

"So you can't even say hi to an old friend?" I jump startled." Tony. Hi. When you get back to town?"" I turn my face away hoping that he doesn't see the bruises. "Oh I been here a few days, and I can see what's been going on with you." I reach up to my face. "Things have been going pretty good. I don't know what happened." He didn't even comment just shook his head. "Will you go somewhere with me? Please?" I want to say something, but I don't need his pity. "Where Tony. I've got to go pick up Keyona and be home by 6:00." I am so sick of just going along with everything and everybody. "Not far. I just want to spend a little time with you." I know that he wants something. "Yeah. Alright. Where's your car?" We go to a motel and Tony treats me the way I deserve to be treated. He takes off my clothes and stares at me. He caresses my body not like I am this big fat girl, but like I am the most beautiful, precious girl in the world. When he takes off his clothes my mind is blown. He has that same carmel color skin from head to toe. I get scared when I see his private part. I guess he could tell because he bent down and kisses me so softly. "Please Connie don't ever be afraid with me, because I will never hurt you." Instantly all my fears go away. I lay back and part my legs for him.

He tries to do things that I never dreamed about, but I am much too shy for that. So he just very slowly sticks it in. He moves ever so slowly. Kissing me all over my face and neck. Telling me how much he loves me. He rides my body for about 2 hours and then it is over. It is like waking up after a beautiful dream. I go to take a shower to wash his beautiful smell off me, and while I am in there I have the saddest thought. For the first time in my life I'm really in love. At least now if Cedric kills me I will have felt that. "Hurry up Connie. Its 5:30 and you still have to go pick up Keyona. I don't want to have to murk that dude if you are late."

* * *

I'm on cloud 20. I haven't felt this good in my life. I wonder when I'm gonna be able to see him again? Even Cedric is smiling at me today. It must really be my lucky day. "You know Connie I been thinking. We've had a pretty rough couple of years, but today has made me see that things are gonna be alright. Let's go on a vacation. I'm sure your grandma would love to keep Keyona for a few days. We never did get to take our honeymoon. Let's take it now." The last thing in the world that I want to do is go away with Cedric. But I really didn't want to spoil his mood so I say, "Yeah honey okay."

For the next 3 months things have been really going good for me. Cedric has stopped beating on me for a while, and I am sneaking off to be with Tony whenever I can.

"Connie? You know I been dreaming about fish lately. You okay?" I stop zipping up Keyonas' jacket. Dreaming about fish? What does that mean? "Of course I'm okay. In fact I've never been better." I don't know why she always asks me silly questions. "When you dream about fish that means someone close to you is pregnant. Are you pregnant?" Not that I know of, but I guess anything is possible.

I go to the doctor the very next day, and sure enough for the second time I am pregnant. Only this time I have a husband, and it is no big deal.

* * *

"Connie are you pregnant?" I turn away so that I can finish fastening my clothes. "Why do you ask me that?" I stand up and stick my feet in my shoes. "Just answer the question. Are you having a baby or not?" I place both my hands on my hips. "Yes Tony. I am pregnant." He gets this excited look on his face. "Is it mine? Cause if it is you are leaving that dude. He ain't gonna stomp the life out of my seed." He looks like he actually believes that it is his. "Of course it's not yours. We always use protection. You know that this is Cedrics' baby." He gets this sheepish look on his face and puts his head down." We haven't always used protection." I start to feel sorry for him. "Oh Tony only the first time we didn't, but that was only 1 time. This baby is Cedrics."

* * *

When I get to be about 5 months along I am huge. Easily the same size I was when I delivered Keyona. "Baby I think something is wrong. You are too big. Are you sure that you are only 5 months?" I look down at my stomach and must admit it scares me how big I am. "I think so, but we are going to have an ultrasound tomorrow." I sit back in my chair. "I'm sho is glad, cause I'm telling you something ain't right."

*  *  *

"Yep Mrs.Scott you're having twins." I almost jump off of that table. "Twins? You mean that there are two babies in me?I groan and roll over onto my side. "Yes. I'm positive you're having twins." Oh my God. What am I going to do now?

"Twins. I knew that something strange was going on. Lord have mercy. How you gon take care of 2 newborns?" My grandmother was happy about it I can tell. "Grandma I don't even know. Shoot I don't even know how I'm gonna tell Cedric. He wasn't thrilled about 1 baby. I'm sure that he's going to turn flips about 2. Maybe he will beat one of them out of me." For the first time in my life I actually play over my food. "Chile don't say that. That's a sin before God. God meant for you to bring twins here, and that's what chu gon do. Now you tell Cedric that I said don't start that foolishness. Lessen he gon have ta deal wit me."

Well it looks like Cedric is gonna have to deal with grandma, cause he is so pissed off. Has been jumping on me every day for the past 2 weeks. All he keeps saying to me is how he gonna take care of 3 kids. He's trying to make me have a miscarriage. I can't let him do that.

\* \* \*

"So you think I'm just gonna let Cedric kill my baby huh?" Tony is furious. "Will you stop saying that? Somebody might here you. You know this is not your baby. Besides it's not just one baby. I'm having twins." I reach for his bag of Skittles "Oh now I know that's all me. Ain't no way that weak, butt dude don shot twins. Ha-Ha." I punch him in the arm and turn to walk away. "Don't worry I'm moving in with my grandparents until the twins are born. Cedric can come over for dinner or company if he gets lonely, but then he has to go back home." It is sad how you can tell that I am actually glad about being away from my own husband for a few months. "Why won't you just leave him? You don't owe that fool nothing." I shake my head. "People have always left him. He just needs someone to love him, and be there for him despite all of his faults. I know what it feels like to really want and need somebody and for nobody to be there." I cross my arms over my chest to let him know that I am serious. "Connie you can't make up for all Cedric didn't have growing up. Other people missed out on those same things, and they aren't beating the hell out of their wives." He really wants me to understand what he is saying. He just didn't understand my loyalty. Oh so I think.

"Tony knowing me the way that you do I would expect you to understand." He pushes my hamburger further into my hands. "I do understand Connie. That's how I know that one day he is going to kill you."

* * *

Being pregnant with twins is the worst experience that I ever had. I didn't even know that my stomach could get that big. And it seems like they would hold hands and do flips inside of me. Tony was absolutely thrilled by the whole thing. Since I was staying with my grandparents I got to sneak out to spend more time with him. No matter what I told him he was totally convinced the twins were his. On the day I was to go to the hospital to have the twins. Tonys truck is parked in front of my grandparents' house. I have to get him out of here before

Cedric showed up. "Tony. What are you doing here?" I am in such a panic "Connie I decided that since these are my babies I'm taking you to the hospital, and I'm watching them come into the world." Tony what are you talking about? I keep telling you these are Cedrics' babies. You are gonna mess up everything if he catches you here. Please I'm begging you to leave before he comes.

"Alright, but after they are born I want a blood test, and if they belong to me you can stay right where you are but they are coming with me." By now I am so frantic I will agree to anything he says. "Okay. Okay. Now please just go." As soon as his truck turns the corner Cedric pulls up. "What are you doing standing out here? Go back inside. You look like you're about to tip over anyway." I'm bending over clutching my sides. "No Cedric. Let's just go to the hospital I think somethings wrong." He throws his car in park before he even speaks. "Dang, can't I get some coffee first? I'm gonna be at the hospital all day." He opens his car door. "Yeah Cedric let's go get you some coffee." Before he opens his mouth I can tell I'm not gonna like whatever he has to say. "I've been thinking. Since we know that we are having a boy and a girl why don't we name them Cedric and

Cedricka? That way I get my Jr. and their names match." That even sounds ugly. "No Cedric. That is horrible. Their names are gonna be Andrew and Andrea. We have already had this discussion." I stand by the door so that he knows not to get comfortable. "Why Connie? I think Cedric and Cedricka are some beautiful names. You got to give Cedric his Jr. anyway." For the first time in my entire life I feel like putting my hands on someone to hurt them. "We already talked about this grandma. Now can we just go before we're late?"

\* \* \*

I woke up hours later to see Cedric sitting across the room holding the twins just staring at them. He looks so proud. One of the babies is jet black with big black curls in its hair. The other one had long, silky straight, black hair and is the prettiest color of carmel. It scares me so bad I hurry up and close my eyes before anyone notices that I am awake. I am so scared. I keep watching the door for Tony to come in with papers requesting a blood test. The more I look at little Cedric the more he looks like Tony. Cedric didn't say anything, but he has the strangest look in his eyes. Soon my 5 days are up and it is time for me to go home. Anybody who has had a baby knows how hard it is with a newborn. Well just imagine that double, and that was my life.

* * *

I can say Cedric did help. If while I am feeding or changing one, and the other one starts to cry Cedric would get up and get it. For the first 6 months of their lives we are almost the perfect little family, but of course all good things must come to an end.

"You stupid fat cow.(slap.) you know this chicken is not done.(Slap.)" I pick myself up off the floor. "I'm sorry. The twins started crying, and I was trying to get them settled then I was gonna finish cooking." I start to run towards the stove. "The twins this. The twins that. I'm tired of these twins. I need to just throw one of the little brats out of the window. Give me that little red one. He doesn't look like he's mine anyway." He reaches for my baby and I snatch him up and start to run down the hall. "No. No. I'll put them in their room." I run upstairs to put the twins in the nursery. Of course Keyona follows me like she is my shadow. Cedric and Cedricka are really fussy, so I decide to sit down in the rocking chair in front of the crib to try and settle them down some. Keyona sits quietly at my feet. I begin to hum a lull-a-bye softly when all of a sudden the door to the nursery slams closed.

All 4 of us jump. I can hear the sound of nails being pounded into the door. I get up and gently lay the babies down into the crib. Walk over to the door, turn the knob, and find the door locked. Cedric be tripping so bad. I start banging on the door. "Cedric. Open this door. Let me out." The twins and Keyona start to cry. "Cedric you are upsetting the kids. Let us out of this room." All of a sudden I notice smoke drifting up from the bottom of the door. "Cedric I know that you are a fool, but not a damn fool. Let us out of here right now. "Connie I can't believe you had the nerve to bring some other man's babies in my house for me to take care of. I can't just put you out, cause if I do you will still be getting away with what you done to me.

So I'm gon make sure that you burn on earth and burn in hell. Along with your demon-seeds." He has set the house on fire. Oh my God. I'm getting ready to die. By now the room is filled with smoke I am about to throw the kids out the window, so at least their lives will be saved. The window isn't big enough for me to fit through, but my kids can fit so at least they will be saved. Then I get an idea. "Keyona.(cough,cough) mommy is going to drop you out of the window. When you get to the ground I want you to go next door and get help as fast as you can." I pick up my baby and drop her out of the second story window. Keyona falls to the ground and crawls next door to get the neighbors. I grab the twins close to my body and sink to the ground. God isn't going to let us die is he? I am lulled into a deep sleep. I wake up to someone grabbing the twins out of my arms, and placing an oxygen mask over my face. We are saved.

Chapter 14

My grandparents finally let me move back home. Keyona has broken both of her legs when I dropped her out of the nursery window, but at least we are finally free of Cedric. I feel kind of sorry for him though. He is in jail waiting to be transferred to a psychiatric hospital. The judge says that he has to be crazy to try and burn down his house with his wife and 3 kids inside. I am so nervous to be back at home. Every time I stand in front of the congregation at my grandfather's church it seems like everyone is staring right at me. I know that they are talking about me, and will be until I am remarried. Tony comes to the rescue just like I knew he would. Exactly one month after my divorce to Cedric is final I marry Tony.

He knew that he couldn't have me any other way. For a wedding present he has me a 5 bdrm. House, 3 baths, and 4 car garage built from the ground up. I even have a swimming pool built down in the ground. I have a ball decorating my home. We have been living out of suitcases, and I can't wait for the day we will move in. I let Tony decorate the outside, and I must admit. Even for a young guy he does a really good job. He even bought me a new truck and a car. He bought himself a car. He put everything in my name. He says he wants me to feel like things are really mine.

\* \* \*

One day Tony asks me if I would do him a favor. I say of course baby what is it? "Well my boy's mother needs a ride up here from Miami." For the first time in our entire relationship he can't look at me. "Can't she fly or take the bus?" I know that he knows how uncomfortable I am driving by semi-trucks. "Uh no she feels better if she comes by car. Baby you just got your truck this would be a good way to open it up. Just pick up Hectors' mom in Miami and drop her off at Jay's moms' house in Detroit." I am really not feeling this, but I don't want him to think that I am ungrateful for all that he has done for me. "What about the kids? Honey that's an awful long drive." I'm trying to think of any excuse that I can. "Don't worry about the kids. They can stay home with me." And there starts my taxi service for Hector and Mrs. Gomez. I would pick her up in Miami, and take her to Detroit, or I would pick her up in Detroit and take her back to Miami. I graduate from Southern University, and Tony throws me a big party. We have the party in our back yard since it looks like a small park. I am standing in the corner talking to some friends when....

"Connie? uh hi. How are you? You did good baby. In school and all." I could not believe it. It is my mother. How she had the nerve to show up at my party is beyond me. "What are you doing here? Who let you in here?" Everybody stops talking to see what is going on. "Baby now I know you're mad at me, but don't mess up your party. I just want to tell you how proud I am..."I can't believe that she even has the gall to be at my party. She has tried to actually kill me several times. "Proud. Proud? Don't you dare use that word and me in the same sentence. You know that you don't care about me. You have never cared about me." I think I am going to pass out. This is actually supposed to be one of the best days of my life and it's turning out to be the worst. Tony walks up and whispers in my ear. "Honey don't do this. Not now. Let me take care of it. I'll fix it. Just please calm down. Look at the kids. They are scared to death. Let me take care of it. I promise that I'll take her away. Baby. You know one day you are going to have to deal with your mother." I cannot believe he is talking to me about that woman. "Tony why would you say such a thing. I am not ever going to have to deal with her. I hate her. And don't want her anywhere near me or my family. She destroys everything she touches. You have no idea about the things she has done to me." I cross my arms across my chest to let him know that the subject is definitely closed. "Connie it doesn't matter. She is still your mother. She told me that she did some things to you that she wasn't proud of, but she also said that she loves you. That she wants to be a part of her grandbabies lives." He places both of his hands on my arms to sort of give me some comfort. "Oh she is not getting near my kids. Especially Cedricka. She will be ruined for life just like I am." Tony gets this puzzled look on his face.

"Why? Tell me the difference between dricka and the other two?" He doesn't get it. He really doesn't understand. Tears run down my face as memories race through my mind. "Don't make me say it. You know the difference. I want to make sure she grows up right." Nobody ever understood. "Baby I don't know what you are talking about. Of course she is going to grow up alright, but why do you think she will have a harder time growing up than Cedric or Keyona?"

I begin to jump up and down and scream at the top of my lungs. "Because she's black that's why. And nobodys gonna like her because she is black." I crumble to the floor. "Oh my God. Is that where all this black stuff comes from? Your mother?" I just start to sob loudly. "Yes. She always made sure I knew about being too black" It is like I opened up a dam. I cannot stop crying. "Oh baby. I am so sorry. Skin color doesn't matter. You are beautiful, and so is Cedricka. Besides how could your mother talk? She's dark too." I begin to just shrug my shoulders. "Yeah, but not like me and not like dricka." My wounds about color are real deep. Tony isn't gonna make me change my mind no matter what he said.

He just didn't understand. How could he? He is light and his skin color is beautiful. "Alright Connie I know that I'm not going to be able to change your mind about skin color, but you have to change your mind about your moms. My mother is dead and gone I would do anything to have her back. You only get 1 mom. I'm not going to let you turn your back on your moms. I think whatever she did to you she is sorry, and I don't think she would ever do anything to our kids. Plus I think she knows enough about me to know that I do not play. I know that she is your moms and all, but if something were to happen to one of our kids...man I don't know." He begins to slowly shake his head. "You're not going to let me turn my back on her. What do you expect me to do?" I look at him like he is absolutely insane. "I don't know, invite her over for dinner. I'll be right here with you. I promise." I can't believe this. He is serous. "She is an evil woman Tony don't you understand that? Anyway I don't know where she lives, so how could I invite her?" I am very upset with her, but I admit. I still love my mother. "Well... you know your moms get high right?" I figured that much.

She use to use drugs when I was little. She shoots up. Use to call it her medicine." I hold my head down, cause now I really get a funny feeling." Well she smokes crack now, but she pretty cool. She don't act like most fiends." She has fooled him too. She fools everybody. "Yes she do. She just got a trick up her sleeve. Even though I haven't seen her in a while I know her."

* * *

"Honey let nana cut up your meat for you. Your mama knows that meat is too big." My mom grabs Keyonas' plate and begins to cut up her meat. "Ma her meat is fine. She just doesn't like to eat meat. Keyona I'm going to beat your butt if you don't eat that food." I stop eating long enough to point my fork at her. "Connie don't holler at her. She gon eat. This steak is delicious. Your grandmother taught you how to cook like this didn't she? Ummm. Yeah this taste just like her steak and gravy." It's really haed for me to get used to her being in my life. Talking about my big momma is the last straw. "Look ma you can cut out all the compliments okay? You know you don't mean them so just stop it." I slam my napkin down on the table "Connie I can't change what I did in the past, but can't we work on something new? I just want to be friends with you and Tony and a grandmother to these kids. Don't worry about the dishes because I'll wash them. I don't know how you keep this big ole house clean and take care of these kids, and got a job.

You need some help, but I'm here now and everything gon be alright. You just watch."

* * *

Everything is alright for about 6 months. Then little things start coming up missing. I didn't want to believe that my mom is stealing from us, but who else could it be? "Ma where is my wallet?"Her face is twitching and her eyes keep darting all around the room. "Where is your what? I know that you are not accusing me of stealing from you." She actually gets down on all fours searching through my carpet. "Ma I just got home. I had my wallet before I got here. Now you can keep the cash just give me back my ID, credit cards, and checkbook." She didn't even have the decency to stop and look at me. "But you don't understand. I need some money Connie." She is curled on the floor like a wounded animal. "Then why don't you ask me for what you need instead of taking my things. You are my mother and I love you. I will always make sure your needs are met." She settles back on her hunches. "Oh so you gon give me some money to buy dope huh? Yeah right." She smacks her lips and tuens away. "If that's what you need so bad that you would steal from me to get it. Yes I will give you money to buy dope. How much do you need we can go get it out the bank right now."

## Chapter 15

Giving my mother money to buy drugs is the worst mistake I ever make. It is never enough and she still steals from me. I have just gotten used to having her around. She cooks and cleans. She even babysits the kids whenever I need her to, but I know that I have to cut her out of my life before Tony finds out about what is going on.

* * *

"What's your car doing out on the block at 1:00 in the morning? Matter of fact what your mama doing with your car period?" I stop tight in my tracks. I have been dreading this conversation. "Aw honey she needed a ride home last night and I didn't feel like bundling the kids up to take them out, so I let her take the car. She should be bringing it back this morning anytime now." He knows that I am lying to him, because I couldn't even look him in the eye. "Wrong I took it from her last night. It's sitting outside. Didn't I tell you she is a dopefiend? You don't give a dopefiend your car and expect to get it back. You think I'm stupid don't you? I know about everything that has been going on around here. I thought you could handle it. Get it under control, but I guess you can't.

Well now your mama is banned from this house. Your mama is banned from my money. Your mama is banned from any car or truck that I paid for. I thought yall could have some kind of relationship, but I was wrong. She just a junkie." Tony is so mad. I have never seen him so angry before, but he is right. Ma quit cooking and cleaning long ago. She is just using me to get money to high just like she did when I was a little girl.

It takes a long time for things to get back to normal. For 1 my mom keeps calling me asking me what she did wrong. Tony tells me that the best thing to do would be to just ignore her, because she will only try to convince me that she didn't do anything.

Tony starts to be away from home more and more. When I ask him what is going on with him, or where he has been he would just tell me that he was taking care of some business. One night before I put the kids to sleep, and of course Tony is out in the streets the front door is kicked in. Men with guns are running in the door screaming for everyone to get down on the ground. I start yelling that I have 3 kids in the house. The kids are yelling and screaming I'm sure scared to death. "ma'am I'm going to tell you 1 more time to get your butt face down on the ground." He points a very big gun right in my face as he says this, "Where is Anthony Duane Smith?" I have no idea what he is talking about. "What? I don't know where Tony is. What's going on?" I didn't think that I could ever be more afraid. "Do you have someone who can pick up your kids?" My eyes got as big around as saucers. "Pick up the kids? Why?" They put handcuffs on me then sat me on the couch. "Okay now Mrs. Smith how do you fit into all this?" When the officer says that I really get surprised. "Fit into all of what?" I start to get butterflies in my stomach turning summersaults. "You do know that Anthony Smith is the biggest dope dealer in town right?" I just close my eyes in complete surrender. "Um... No, I didn't know that." The crazy route is the best one to take now. "Come on you..." Before he can even finish his sentence another one of the police officers with him comes up the stairs from the basement. "Chief you need to take a look at what we found down here." After the man who the other officers are calling the chief walks down the stairs. After he gets down there I can hear excited talking then afterwards dead silence. The chief walks up the stairs and right over to me. "You need to make arrangements for these kids before I do, because you are coming with me."

Riding in the back of that police car I am so angry. I just couldn't imagine how Tony could do this to us. And where is he? When I get my hands on him I am going to kill him. I wonder where they are taking me. It doesn't look like we are anywhere near the jail. Oh shoot. What if they aren't really police officers? What if what they really want is to rob me? Oh my God. Lord please help me. Don't let these men kill me. Why are we on the highway? Where am I going? Tony will never be able to find me. I ain't never gonna see my kids again.

After a while I could see that we are pulling up to a jail, but we are in some other town. I didn't get it, but at least I really am with the police and wasn't getting ready to die. We go inside and they just put me in a cell. They didn't take off my handcuffs or nothing. I am so tired. I just lay down on the floor and go to sleep. I smell piss everywhere.

* * *

The puke green walls are the first thing that I see when I open my eyes. My head hurts.

My face is lying on the cold, concrete floor. Where am I? My hands are handcuffed behind my back. I feel like my shoulder is about to pop out of socket. I wish somebody would take these handcuffs off. "Hey. Can anybody hear me? Hey." I can hear a girl call out from probably another cell somewhere. "Girl you might as well be quiet. We can all hear you, but nobody gives a damn what you got to say." I try to sit up. "Who said that?" The walls start spinning, so I just lay back down. I close my eyes and try to get myself together before I speak. "Do you think somebody will come take these handcuffs off? They're too tight, and my arm hurts really bad". I can't believe I got myself into this."Look girl, we all got problems. Right now my biggest one is a headache that ain't getting no better with you screaming your head off. They will come take the cuffs off when they feel like it. You in jail, so all you got is time. Just relax." I realize that she is probably right, and settle down. Try to get as comfortable as I can.

"Smith. Smith. You got a visit." Praise the Lord. I'm getting ready to get out of here. He comes into the cell to remove my handcuffs. It's like my arms are screaming they are so happy. "Yeah, yeah praise the Lord. We happy too." We walk down this long hallway into the visiting room. Tony is sitting behind this glass with this big kool-aid smile on his face like I should be happy to see him. He taps on the glass and gestures for me to pick up the phone on my side of the glass.

"Tony. What in the world is going on?? Why am I in jail? What was in that room in the basement?" Actuallt I don't even care what he has got to say. I'm just glad that he is here and will straighten this mess all out. "Baby calm down. Just calm down. I'm sorry about everything that happened, but it's gonna be alright. I promise. Have you talked to anybody yet?" I can't believe it. What about me, and why I'm in this place in the first place. "No. They left me in a cell with handcuffs on all night." I try to be angry, but truth be told I'm just happy to see him. "They just trying to scare you. Now baby I need you to listen to me. I might not be able to see you again for a while." My balloon is really busted now. What is he talking about? "What are you talking about? I'm not getting ready to get out of here?" Oh my God he is serious. "Baby please just listen. Do not talk to these people. Do you understand me? Do not say one word to them. When they start asking you questions just say quiet. They do not got nothing on you, and you have never been in trouble before so the most they can do to you if anything is give you probation. Now they are gonna try to get you to talk about me, but baby listen to me. If you do they are gonna get me and put me in prison for life. Do you hear me? LIFE. Don't let them trick you baby. We have to stick together. Ima send a lawyer down here to talk to you. Just remember don't say nothing.

They can't do anything to you. Don't worry about nothing I got everything taken care of. When you get out of here me, you, and the kids are moving to Detroit. I put money on your books. I love you baby. Don't ever forget that." Then he just walked out. At first I was scared, but now that Tony has explained things to me I know what to expect. I am fine now. I am ready. At least I think I am.

* * *

"Okay Mrs. Smith. My name is Detective Wright. Now have they advised you of your rights? How are they treating you in here?" He is looking all smug. He just doesn't know Tony has already told me what to expect he might as well stop trying to act like my friend. I am not buying it. "They are treating me just fine. When am I getting out of here?" I plop in my seat and cross my arms across my chest. "Well I don't know, but agent Snow might be able to tell you in a minute. I just wanted to come in here first and make sure you are alright. Do you want me to get you anything?" I couldn't believe it. He really thinks I'm stupid. Well I'm going to show him. "No. I just want to go home." I poke my lips out in a pout. "Well Mrs. Smith I've seen so many young girls like you. Just please. Please cooperate with Agent Snow. Tell him what he wants to know, and go home." He looks at me so pitiful. "I ain't telling yall nothing. I ain't got nothing to say. "I roll my eyes to let them know that I am serious. Just then the door opens and another officer walks in. "Mrs. Smith? What's happening? My name is Agent Snow." I couldn't believe it. Jay? "You're a police officer? You go with my friend Shannon. Does she know you're a cop?" Jay looks at me with the saddest eyes. "Look Connie, I ain't getting ready to yank your chain. Yes. You know me as Tonys' best friend Jay.

I have been undercover for a long time. We really want Tony. He is such a bad guy. We have been trying to get him for a very long time. We believe you can help us do that. If you help us then the cases for the money, dope and guns we found in your house goes away. If you don't help us your kids will be grown by the time you get out." I can't believe that he actually has the nerve to say that to me. "I can't help you. I don't know nothing." Tony is right even his own best friend is out to get him. "Yes you do. Who is the lady that you picked up several times in Florida and brought to my house? What is her address? How do we get in touch with Hector?" I ain't telling him nothing. He may not be a loyal friend to Tony, but I'm going to show him that I am. "I don't know. I don't know, and I don't know." I don't know what they are trying to do. All I know is that I have to protect Tony. If he is such a bad guy then so was Jay. They were together all the time. Tony told me that they were going to try and trick me. "Jay you were with Tony more than I was. As a matter of fact you were with Tony when I met him.

Are you sure that you don't know the answers to your own questions? Tony loves you. Why are you doing this to him?" Jay looks at me for a long time. Then he says, "You're gonna go down for him aren't you? He told me the first time he ever laid eyes on you that you were the one he needed. He knew that you would take the hit for him. Connie you're a damn fool to choose this man over your own kids. It doesn't matter what he told you. It'a all a lie. You're gonna go to prison for a long time. All for nothing." He slowly just shakes his head. "That's where you're wrong Jay. It won't be for nothing. It'll be for love." I tip my head back in defiance. "Yeah, that's nice except he doesn't love you."

\* \* \*

"Mrs. Annette Smith. I'm gonna accept your guilty plea. Are you ready for sentencing?" Was I ready? I have been ready. I know that I am gonna get to go home today. Tony told me that all they could give me is probation, and I am ready for it. I have had enough jail. "Mrs. Smith even though this is your very first time in a court of law. I am simply appalled by your crime. You have been making a ton of money off the misfortune of others. Did you ever stop to think about the lives you were destroying with your poison? I know that you have small children, so I'm going to ask you this: Did you ever think about the children's lives you were destroying with your poison? I think not. I am going to set an example with you so others will think twice before breaking these same laws. I hereby sentence you to 300 months at the federal correctional institution in Danbury Connecticut... blah, blah, blah..." 300 months. What is that? I'm only supposed to get probation. I look back towards the seats in the courtroom. My grandmother is crying hysterically. Way in the back row. I can see Jay just shaking his head slowly. He gets up and walks out of the courtroom. Well Tony is my husband and my best friend. What are best friends for?

300 months? What is that? How much time is that? When I find out that it is 25 years I begin screaming at them to wait a minute. I turn around and look at my grandmother holding my twins with tears streaming down her face. I didn't know what she is crying for. I am the one on my way to prison. I'm surprised that she isn't on her knees moaning and praying. Where is her God now? I knew it. All that holiness is just crap. Now that I really need it. Where is it? My kids must have felt something because the twins start to cry and Keyona starts to wave good-bye. I look in the back of the courtroom while the deputy is leading me out the room and see Jay just sitting there. He too had tears running down his face, but he is slowly shaking his head. I didn't get it. Why is everybody crying? Tony is my best friend. That's what you are supposed to do for a friend right? Right? That's what you're supposed to do for your friends....

## Chapter 16

I am sitting in the shower room with about 19 other naked women. I have never felt more humiliated in my whole life. They take all of our clothes even our underwear. They even cut this one girls weave out. Another girls eyes changed colors right in front of me when they took her contacts out. "Alright. I want all you ballerinas to get up, spin around on your toes, bend over and spread em." As black as I know that I am all the color drains out of my face. Spread em? Spread what? I look around, and women are bending over holding their butt cheeks apart. I think I am going to die right then. "Home girl you are gonna have to just do whatever it is that you have to do, because there is no way in hell that I am doing that." I sit down in the folding chair.

"Inmate what did you say to me? First of all I'm not your home girl. Save that for your little girlfriends on the yard. And if you don't bend over and spread em right now I promise that you won't like it if I come over there and do it for you." I can't believe she is talking to me like this. Tears silently roll down my face. I get up, and turn around and bend over. I am so humiliated. I just want it to hurry up and be over. The lady spread my vaginal lips and butt cheeks so hard, and it hurt so bad. What in the world do they think I would hide up inside me?

After all of us have been thoroughly searched we are led over to the clothing issue room. We are issued: 4-washcloths,4-towels,4-khaki shirts,4-khaki pants,4-chocolate brown t-shirts,5 pr.panties,5-bras,5-pr. Of sock, 1-pillowcase, 2-sheets, and 2-blankets. Also a pillow. We are taken to 3 different units. I am housed in unit 9. When I walk into my room there is a girl lying on the top bunk. "Hey what's your name? Dang you black. I ain't never seen nobody as black as you. Are you from Africa?" No. I'm not. I'm from right here in America. My name is Connie what's your name? "Everybody should call you blackie. Ha-Ha-Ha. Naw, I'm just kidding. My name is Nina. How long you got?" 300 months I have mumble to myself.

Nina rolls right off the bed onto the floor. Hey are you okay? "Yeah. I'm straight. I thought you said that you have 300 months." I lower my head. "I did" I say this so softly that I can bare "Dang. What did you do? That's 25 years. Don't tell me that you are a cho mo." I look at her she has lost her mind. "What's a cho mo?" A know for sure that I have got to get this prison lingo down. "A child molester" Oh my of course not that. "Uh no I'm not a cho mo. I was put in here for conspiracy." I almost whisper "Crack? You in here for selling that yayo?" She jumps down. "I wasn't selling anything" I am not like these other people in this place. "Well you shoulda been. Cause you sho finna do this time like you was selling it. Ha-Ha-Ha. You might as well learn how to crochet, or knit. That's what everybody with baby life does. Ha-Ha-Ha." What is so funny? There is nothing funny about getting this time. "Baby life? What's that?" I'm dead serious "Um the joke is on you cause it's your sentence." I just sit down on my bunk without even making it up. I could hear Nina up over me talking, but what she is saying I can't tell you. How am I going to do 25 years?? I'm barely over 20 years old. Bad stuff has been happening to me my entire life, and I've had it.

I guess I know for a fact that there ain't no God. If it is He would have never let all this bad stuff happen to me. 1 thing maybe. 2 things maybe, but all the things that have happened to me in my life back to back? Come on now. "Hey Connie. Did you hear what I just said? "Yes Nina

I hear you." I have absolutely no idea what she just said. "So you agree when I said that a purple elephant was at the door?" This time I sit up and pay attention. "A purple what? Okay. I might as well come clean. I could hear you talking, but I wasn't listening. My mind was on how I'm gonna do all this time." She just chuckles softly. "I can tell you how I just did this dime I got. One day at a time. I'm going home on Monday, and I promise you that there were plenty times that I thought I wouldn't make it. 10 years was just too much time to wrap my young mind around." I couldn't believe what she just said to me. "You think you are young? When I came I was 19. I was mad at the whole world. Especially God..." I had to stop this right now. "Let me stop you right there. If you are getting ready to start preaching that God stuff I'm telling you right now I'm leaving. I have heard enough about this wonderful God to last me a lifetime." I turn over on my side to let her know that I don't want to talk about this anymore.

"I might as well just tell you upfront I don't buy it. He's not real. I just have had it with all this God stuff. If God is real how come he doesn't love me? I have never done anything to Him, but He has let crazy stuff happen to me all of my life. I'll even do you 1 better. My granddaddy is a preacher, and I just got sentenced to 25 years for nothing. You hear me? For nothing. I jump up and run out of the room. I had to get away from this silly girl for a minute. She maybe older than me in years, but she had a lot to learn. She said that she just finished doing 10 years? She hasn't learned yet?

## Chapter 17

"Connie. Help me. Please Connie don't let me die. Please not yet. I'm going home in the morning. My daughter is waiting on me. I promised. I promised." At first I think I am dreaming. After about 1 minute I realize that I wasn't dreaming after all. I slowly stand up, and what I see when I did took my breath away. Nina is lying on her back with about 10 shanks stuck in her body. I am frozen. She is dying and there is absolutely nothing I could do about it. We have been bunkies for 3 days. She has taught me all the ins and outs of prison. Shown me how to make a cook-up and even a cheesecake out of creamer. What am I going to do without her? As soon as I say these words she takes a big breath and exhales for the last time. NO... Our officer working the unit runs into our room.

It takes him and two other officers to pull me away from Nina's' body. Lieutenant Gonzalez pulls me into the office to calm me down. "You've had a pretty intense 1st weekend huh?" I'm sitting down in the chair with my heart just broken. "Yeah. I'll be okay. I just keep thinking about Ninas' family. She is supposed to go home in the morning. "I start to rub my own arms. "Yeah. I heard about that. I guess that's a pretty good lesson for you to learn right away. Some of these ladies in this place have a long sentence or even life. So it's not a good idea to brag about an outdate. "I laugh quietly to myself. "Well I've got a 20 year sentence, so that definitely won't be a problem." He runs his hand over his head. "Ha-Ha-Ha. If you look at it that way I guess you're right, but tell me? What are you going to do? How are you going to survive 20 years, and make sure that you do make it someday?" I take in a deep breath. Lieutenant to be honest with you. I probably won't make it home. My out date isn't until 2013. You and I both know that the world is going to end in 1999." He burst out laughing "So if you really believe that. What are you going to do for the next 5 years?" He thinks he's so smart. I've got something for him.

"I have always dreamed of being the bad girl that everybody thinks I am, so for starters..." I cock my arm back and punch her right in the mouth. I vow to myself right then and there that I wasn't going to be close to anyone else. I am so mad, and it is time for someone to pay. I am ready to jump right on top of her, but all of a sudden the office door slams open, and about 10 male officers pin me to the floor. They still had to taze me in the rear to get me to stop fighting them. Over the next 13 years I was tazed 3 more times, and placed in the SHU a total of 22 more times. It is like a light switch had been flipped off. For as far back as I could remember I have been sucking on sour lemons. And for what?? Nothing that's what. In the special housing unit they have built a special cell for me, because I have a filthy habit of throwing out urine and feces on the officers when they make their rounds. It is surrounded by plexi-glass so that the officers could see everything I was doing, but I couldn't dash anything on them. Most of the time they turned off the water in the cell. The only piece of furniture in the cell is a combination toilet and sink. They always take my clothes as well, because if I wasn't trying to harm them I am trying to harm myself.

* * *

One day I think it is a day I have been in that cell so long I couldn't tell. I had had it. I am hurting so bad. I really am not even sure if there is a God or not, but I figure I'd give it a shot. I roll over onto my back. "Hey. I don't know if you are up there or not but if you are you better come down here and save me right now." Now I would love to say the thunder rolled and the lightening flashed. That the cell door opened, but none of that happened. What did happen is a sense of peace that I have never felt before flows over my entire body. This time when the tears roll down my face they weren't sad tears. They are happy tears. I finally understood what that song I learned as a little girl meant. Jesus did love me. Not like those grown men who hurt me, when I was a child or even Cedric or Tony.

Jesus didn't love me like my granddaddy did. He loves me when I am angry and mean, throwing pee and doo doo on people. Cussing and fighting other people. Something strange starts happening. I had read the Bible about 10 times at least in my life, but I felt like I need to read it again. I couldn't even begin to guess what is going on. "Hey. Help me. I'm going crazy down here." I start banging on the bars. "Are you just figuring that out? Ha-Ha-Ha. We guessed that a long time ago. Why do you think we have you in this cage right here?" He laughs. I lunge towards the cell door.    "I ain't in no cage. You hear me. I'm never going in a cage again." I grab hold to the bars and begin to rattle them. "Okay Joness just settle down. Do you want me to call the doctor?" The officer instinctively reaches for his walkie-talkie. "No. please don't call the doctor. I need to see the chaplain." When I say that it is like all the wind goes out of my sail. "Chaplain? The last time the chaplain was down here you talked to her so bad. She said that she was never coming back." He leans against the wall opposite my cell door.

"Im sorry. Please tell her that I'm sorry. I need to talk to her so bad." Tears begin to roll down my face. "Alright, alright. If you promise to settle down I'll call her." He stands up straight and points his finger in my face. "I'll be good. I'll settle down." I begin jumping up and down like a little kid. "Well I don't have to leave today to go home and take a shower, so that is a step in the right direction at least." The C.O. walked away from the front of my cell. He wasn't gonna call the chaplain. I lie down in the corner and fall directly to sleep."

* * *

"Connie? Inmate Joness? You requested to see me? What's wrong now?" I open my eyes to see chaplain Hurd standing at the door of my cell. "Chaplain. Help me. I'm going crazy." I sit up and almost run to the front of the cell. "Of that I have no doubt, but what do you want with me? How do you think talking to me will help you?" Chaplain I'm saved. He's real. God is real.

The chaplain just looks at me with this blank look on her face. I know that she didn't believe me, but I have to try to make her understand what happened to me. "Chaplain I know that you have heard this many times before, but God really did come into this cell with me and I believe. I believe." I grab a hold of the bars, and lean in. "What do you believe Ms. Joness? Do you want to file a complaint against God now? You say that he was in your cell with you? Did he touch you?" I sadly shake my head. She didn't believe me.

"No? Well at least that's good. Are you going to throw some body fluids on me today?" Now she looks almost bored. "No. I'm not. Look chaplain it doesn't look like anybody is going to believe me about really getting saved, but everybody will see. I'll just have to show them or you all rather." With that being said I just laid back down in my corner. Trying to focus on what I am really going to do with my life now. I am so excited to see what was going to happen next.

Chapter 18

I thought the people around me would be as excited about my transformation as I was, but they weren't. They were just happy that I wasn't throwing poop on them anymore. People had noticed that I was different though. They just didn't actually agree with me as to why. They did give me some clothes to wear finally, and put me in a regular cell after a while. "Good morning Connie. I brought you something that you have been asking for." I look over at the door and see the chaplain standing there. "Good morning chaplain Hurd.

What did you bring me?" At first I am almost too embarrassed to ask. "Do you still want a bible?" I sign in relief. I am so excited. "Yes." "Well I brought you one today. Now remember you promised to behave." I start reading it before I even sit down. "I remember. I'll behave. I was so excited. Yesterday a shower and today a Bible. It's funny how we can appreciate the simple things in life if they are with-held long enough.

* * *

The committee told me that they are going to review my case in 120 days, and if I am still doing well they will release me back to general population. I don't even care. I am just happy that I have at least another 4 months to talk to this new God that I am getting to know.

He isn't the God that my grandmother had introduced me to many years ago, or the God that my grandfather had preached about when I was growing up that was going to get me if I didn't be good. This God loves me and I don't have to be good. Jesus died on the cross for all the things that I ever thought that I would do. For the next 4 months I spent all of my time learning about the God of my own understanding. It was like learning all about God for the first time.

* * *

"Connie, how are you doing today? I want to talk to you about going to another prison where we have this faith based program. For the past 31/2 months I have watched you diligently study the Bible, and this program will answer a lot of the questions that I'm sure you have. So what do you think? I also think going to a new place where people don't know you will be a good fresh start for you. I think that it will also show the committee that you are serious about changing." At first I am kind of thrown off by her interrupting my Bible study time, but after I hear what she has to say I'm all ears. "Chaplain I think that is a great idea. Yes. Yes. I'll go." What she didn't know this is actually a release. "Ha-Ha-Ha. Okay Connie I'll start the paperwork. I'll also put in a good word for you with the committee." I can't believe it. She is serious. "Chaplain I didn't want to say anything , but do you think they will let me out this time?" I bite on my lip, because now I'm nervous. "To be honest with you Connie I hope they don't until we can get you on a plane out of here." What she doesn't know is I think the same thing. "You know what Chaplain? If you want me to be honest with you I don't either. I've done so much bad stuff to people here if they make me go back out there to the compound people are going to be trying to try me, and yes I love the Lord for real,

But turn the other cheek? I ain't there yet." I cross my arms and roll my eyes. "Ha-Ha-Ha no Connie I didn't think you were. I'm praying though, and I'd be willing to bet one day you will be." That night I can hardly sleep. I am going in front of the committee in the morning. I want to get out of segregation, but I just wasn't sure that they were going to let me.

* * *

"Good morning Ms. Joness. I'm assistant warden Johnson. This is the classification committee: Mr.Daly, unit manager Stevens, counselor Smith, Officer Johnson, and Chaplain Hurd." My mouth drops open. Chaplain Hurd was on the committee? She never even told me. When AW Johnson told me that I was being shipped to Mobile, Texas to general population I didn't hear him at first. "Excuse me Mr. Johnson. You're letting me out of the hole?" I am almost afraid to ask. "Yes Ms. Joness we are. This committee believes in you. Especially Chaplain Hurd. I hope you don't let us all down." I can't believe it. They are really going to let me out.

"AW I won't.. I drop to my knees right there, and began thanking God for my deliverance. Even though the committee is putting me back in general population I have to remain in the hole until my transfer. I didn't mind at all. Was I nervous? Extremely. But for the first time in my life I know deep down in my heart that God is going to work all things together for my good. All of my life I never thought I was good enough, pretty enough. For the first time when I look in the mirror I see the glow of the Lord shining out. Now I can say without a shadow of a doubt that I'm glowing. I'm really glowing.

## Chapter 19

Mobile Texas was a big change for me. The weather for one was different than anything I've ever encountered. It was either horribly hot, or tornado season. Also just because I had sided with the Lord that did not mean that life was going to be smooth sailing for me. It was like the devil had me on his hit list all of a sudden. Temptations that I never saw coming, or ever even had a problem with before all of a sudden were coming at me from all directions. I was bound and determined not to get into it with anybody, but what do thcy say about good intentions?

\* \* \*

"Move out of my way blackie." It was like I was that scared little girl all over again. "Blackie is not my name. You can call me Joness like everybody else." She walks into my personal space and points her finger "I ain't calling you nothing but what I see, and all I see is a big blob of black. So I guess I'll be calling you blackie." With that being said she punched me right in the mouth. At first I just laid on the ground. Now God knew that I was trying to do the right thing. I wasn't trying to get in any fights here. But I wasn't finna let nobody hit me and get away with it either.

I jump up before I even know it, and start swinging. I am swinging for old and new. I had had it. I really am sick of being everyone's' punching bag. Yeah I believe in God, but I wasn't just going to let people punk me out because I believe in God. I am not going to be taken advantage of anymore. This girl is getting ready to get beat down for young me and old me. I grab a hold of that girls ears and just start slamming her head into the ground. "I have been waiting for this side of you to show up." The sgt. Pointed the taser at me and pulled the trigger. The pain exploded down the right side of my body.

It brought me back to myself it hurt so bad. Okay I give up I yell. "Get down on the ground with your hands behind your head." As I lay on the ground with my face in the dirt tears are just running down my face. I thought that I had changed. I am on my way back to the hole once again. Only this time I donn't want to go. I don't want to be caged up like an animal. I ain't an animal. For the first time I don't want to be treated like one either.

* * *

"Alright take off all your clothes and place them in this bag and put on this jumpsuit." I know the drill. As I change into my SHU clothes I realize that this is the last time I am going to be placed in a place like this. I allow myself to be handcuffed and led to my cell for the final time. When I am placed in my cell I jump as my cell door clanged shut. I back up to place my wrists through the feed slot, so the handcuffs could be removed. After the officer slams the feed slot closed I drop to my knees.

I cried out to God like I did the day He came into my heart. I told Him all about all of the things that had been bothering me (like He didn't already know.) I stay on my knees crying out to the Lord for hours. "Ey inmate. Are you gonna come get this food, or not? Personally I hope all of yall starve yourselves to death. Less work for me to have to do." I can remember a time when I would have gotten smart about a comment like that. Not this time. I just look up at the officer.

"Excuse me sir. I didn't hear you open the slot. I think that I'm going to pass on dinner tonight. I think I could stand to lose a few pounds. Don't you? "A few? Maybe a hundred." He slams the slot closed. I get up off the floor and sit on my bunk. I need to figure out what I am going to do with me. How am I going to make sure that I never come back to a place like this? Wanting my life to change is great, but change to what? If I didn't find something positive to replace all the garbage in my life I may as well get used to being in this SHU, cause that is what is going to end up happening.

## Chapter 20

I end up staying in the SHU for 45 days. Now I walk around the track in the mornings for a couple of hours, work-out in the gym in the evenings. Attend all the Bible study classes that I can. I don't go into the tv room anymore. I don't play cards anymore. Anything that could make me revert back to my old ways is taken out of my life. I'm getting ready to go home. I never thought that I would live to see the day that I get to go home. I know today that He didn't allow me to go through all the things that I have gone through in my life for nothing. He has a large ministry planned for me.

I know that now and have to concentrate on making myself believe that no I'm not worthy. Nobody is, but Jesus is, and God is looking at me through the blood of Jesus. If I thought I was glowing before I know that I am today.

## ACKNOWLEDGEMENTS

First and foremost I would like to thank God, cause without Him? I never would have made it.

My 3 children Achia, Willie and Willesha. I love you with all of my heart.

Deja, Ramee,Jacuez,Parker,Dani,Brooklyn and Jaymi my precious grandbabies always remember all that I do is for you.

My best friend and big sister Joy. Thanks for always being there. Through the good and bad times.(Mostly bad!) But now? Good times! These are the good times!

Pastor Kenneth Jones Jr. and my church family Como First Missionary Baptist Church. Thanks for giving me the chance to really glow.

Minister Ella Burton I will never be able to express in mere words how very much you mean to me. Just know that when I grow up I want to be just like you!!!!!

I know that I dedicated this novel to Sandra Stanley, but that was to Sandra Stanley the director of Opening Doors For Women In Need, But this is a very sincere thank you to the woman Sandra Stanley, the mentor, mother, grandmother and most down to earth woman of

God that I ever met. I have always thought that I was the original girl that glows, but actually it is you! A special thanks for all that you do.

Now to my readers this journey has been truly humbling and thanks for the ride. Until next time!!!!!!

Be Blessed!!!!

*Onyx*